W9-DFF-324

DISCARD

I've travelled the world twice over,
Met the famous: saints and sinners,
Poets and artists, kings and queens,
Old stars and hopeful beginners,
I've been where no-one's been before,
Learned secrets from writers and cooks
All with one library ticket
To the wonderful world of books.

© JANICE JAMES

WAITING FOR WILLA

A suspense novel set in Stockholm as winter settles down on the city and its surrounding forests. As soon as Grace saw that her cousin's letter was signed 'Wilhelmina' she scented trouble. Since their schooldays, this full name that Willa hated had been a secret call for help. Willa was gay, impulsive, extrovert; Grace was the introvert and the rescuer. When no reply came to her cable to Willa, Grace was sufficiently worried to fly to Sweden, only to find that Willa had disappeared.

*Books by Dorothy Eden in the
Ulverscroft Large Print Series:*

THE BIRD IN THE CHIMNEY
THE SLEEPING BRIDE
THE SHADOW WIFE
BRIDE BY CANDLELIGHT
NIGHT OF THE LETTER
THE VOICE OF THE DOLLS
WHISTLE FOR THE CROWS
LISTEN TO DANGER
THE TIME OF THE DRAGON
AFTERNOON FOR LIZARDS
THE PRETTY ONES
SIEGE IN THE SUN
WINTERWOOD
DEATH IS A RED ROSE
THE DEADLY TRAVELLERS
THE MARRIAGE CHEST
WAITING FOR WILLA

DOROTHY EDEN

WAITING FOR WILLA

Complete and Unabridged

ULVERSCROFT
Leicester

First Printed 1970

First Large Print Edition
published October 1979
by arrangement with
Hodder & Stoughton Ltd
London
and
Coward, McCann & Geoghegan, Inc
New York

British Library CIP Data

Eden, Dorothy
  Waiting for Willa. — Large print ed.
  (Ulverscroft large print series:
    romantic suspense)
  I. Title
  823'.9'1F   PR6055.D4W/

ISBN 0-7089-0356-8

Published by
F. A. Thorpe (Publishing) Ltd
Anstey, Leicestershire
Printed in England

Love is
a time of enchantment:
in it all days are fair and all fields
green. Youth is blest by it,
old age made benign: the eyes of love see
roses blooming in December,
and sunshine through rain. Verily
is the time of true-love
a time of enchantment—and
Oh! how eager is woman
to be bewitched!

1

THE sombre Swedish countryside tipped beneath the wings of the plane, endless spruce forests lighted at intervals by autumn-tinted birches, outcrops of rocks like bare bones, small dark red houses that looked as if they had been dropped haphazardly into the forest.

It was too late to read Willa's letter again. In any case Grace almost knew it by heart. The first page was Willa's account of life in Stockholm written in her usual compulsive way. The people she had met, the parties she had been to, the kind of food the Swedes ate, even the weather—it was all treated with drama.

Willa, with her skinny body and sharp eager face had always wanted to be larger than life so she made all the events with which she was associated subjects of exaggerated importance.

She was very different from herself, Grace thought, with her sober ways. Though only Grace knew the tension that lay beneath

Willa's gaiety and her uniform of eccentric hair styles and daring clothes.

That was why, after reading her apparently happy letter, Grace had felt the shock of the last brief paragraph.

'*All the same, I must tell you that a situation has developed. Don't say, doesn't it always, because this one is different. I've made a decision, but I'm not sure if it's the right one. Yet there is simply no other way . . .*

Wilhelmina'

And there was the crux of the matter. When they were in their teens, and had been sent to different boarding schools, Grace and Willa had made a pact that if Willa was in trouble (it was never suggested that Grace might be in trouble) she would sign her full name, the old-fashioned Wilhelmina which she hated, to a letter. Wilhelmina. Thus, a secret cry for help could be made.

It was a fanciful schoolgirl arrangement that they hadn't used for years. Grace had almost forgotten about it until the letter from Stockholm had arrived. The unfamiliar 'Wilhelmina' scrawled across the page had made her heart give a sharp jump of apprehension. What was this mysterious situation that had developed, and why couldn't Willa, with her usual engaging deviousness, get out of it?

GRACE KEPT the letter for a week, uncertain what to do, hoping that another would quickly follow, explaining that cry for help. She would like to have asked advice of somebody. There were, after all, several people only too anxious to give her advice about anything that troubled her. Her publishers, who were personal as well as business friends, her father, a few other friends of hers and Willa's, would all have been delighted to interpret this enigmatic letter.

Grace's mother and Willa's, who had been identical twins and closer to one another than they had ever been to their respective husbands or their daughters, had died within months of one another, their mysterious alliance drawing them together even in their graves.

It had been agreed between Grace and Willa, however, that if the code were used, it was intended as a secret. Otherwise why bother to use it? So it was obvious that whatever trouble Willa might be in, she intended it to be known to no one but Grace.

One might ask oneself, why didn't Willa write, 'Can you come?' She knew that Grace was in the unsettled between-books stage. She had frequently written during the summer that Grace must come and stay with her as soon as she had finished her current book. She had a nice flat on Strandvagen, the street that overlooked the harbour, and which had a wonderful view of the palace and the buildings in the old town. One thing about Embassy work, a girl got enough money to live decently. If she had remained in London it would have been a bed-sitter in the Fulham Road, which would have been galling, considering that Grace was now beginning to make a respectable income from her books. For all their devotion to each other, the cousins were highly competitive. Grace had wondered lately whether her own modest fame was making Willa exaggerate the dramas in her life, even whether she were deliberately creating dramas.

Whatever the reason for the letter, something had to be done about it. Grace sent off a telegram, DONT UNDERSTAND YOUR LETTER TELL ME MORE, and when, after a week, no answer had come, she was in a state of sufficient anxiety to buy an air ticket to Stockholm. She telegraphed again, the date and time of her arrival, and now she was here.

She was a quietly intense anxious kind of person who did not do things on the spur of the moment. All the same, it was rather fun to be embarked on a wild goose chase. If that was what this was. For she was sure Willa would be waiting on the other side of the barrier, screaming, "Grace! How perfectly marvellous!"

The air was unexpectedly cold and frosty. A sharp wind was blowing across the landing field. Grace wrapped her coat about her, thinking how quickly the warm muggy air of England had turned into this northern wintriness. The sky was pale and clear, with a pink tinge on the horizon. One began to think of Finland and Lapland and ice floes and the north star, and it was suddenly exciting. She was glad she had come. She had no doubt at all about Willa's welcome.

Except that Willa was not at the airport to greet her.

A row of stolid Swedes, wrapped in heavy coats and mufflers, hats pulled down over pale indoor faces, stood beyond the barrier.

5

There was no one there even faintly resembling Willa, taking into account that one didn't know the hair colour she currently favoured, or whether she had dressed herself in unfamiliar tweeds.

No one.

Grace listened to the immigration officer's impeccable English.

"You are on holiday, Miss Asherton?"

"Yes."

The rubber stamp came down on her passport.

"*Tak*. Have a good time."

No one to meet her. The airport bus filled with strangers. The long drive through the bleak countryside to the city. The traffic thickening, little speeding Volvos and Mercedes and Saabs. A long narrow cemetery filled with tall dark pine trees that dwarfed the grey tombstones, painted gilded graceful gates leading to a palace, modest skyscrapers in the distance. Then the air terminal, and a gloomy-faced taxi driver to take one to Willa's flat on Strandvagen.

The door of the slim dark red house facing the harbour was opened by a stout woman whose pale blue eyes had faded to colourlessness. They were round and protruding like cabochon-cut agates. They gave their owner a look of overwhelming coldness, although her voice was polite and even reasonably friendly.

"Do you speak English?" Grace asked, and when the woman answered yes, a little, she said, "Does Miss Willa Bedford live here?"

"She does, but she is absent at present. Was she expecting you?"

"I'm not sure. Do you know where she is?"

"*Nej*. She did not tell me where she was going. Come in. The wind is cold."

Grace stepped into the narrow stone-floored hall. There was a steep flight of stairs (a walk-up, Willa had called her flat), a board on the dark brown wall with a list of names, presumably of tenants, and a table with some unclaimed mail.

"I am Fru Lindstrom," the woman said. "You are a friend of Froken Bedford's?"

"Yes, her cousin. Grace Asherton. I sent her a telegram a few days ago but she didn't answer it."

The woman pounced, extracting an envelope from the unclaimed mail.

"This? It is here still. Undelivered because Froken Bedford has not returned."

Grace frowned.

"Did she tell you how long she would be away?"

"Not a word. She took a small bag and departed."

"When?"

"Let me think—perhaps ten days since."

About the time she had written that letter to Grace. *A situation has developed . . .*

"But she is coming back, of course."

"I should expect so. She still has her apartment. I understand the rent is paid until the end of the year. I think she would hardly give all that up so carelessly."

"No, I'm sure she wouldn't. Do you have a key to the apartment, Mrs. Lindstrom? Could I go up?"

"Certainly. You are welcome. I am glad you have come. I was a little—"

"Worried?" Grace said instinctively.

The woman shook her head. "Puzzled, perhaps. There is such silence, you see. Froken Bedford was not a silent young woman before."

"She used to tell you things?"

"That's what I mean. First, she was always chattering. Then lately she was silent. Then she came downstairs with her bag and said she would be away for a short time, and

8

what a lucky thing she hadn't got a bird."

"A bird!"

Fru Lindstrom gave a surprisingly jolly smile.

"She was going to get a canary to sing. Her room was too quiet, she said. She liked noise. I expect you know."

Grace nodded, agreeing. Willa liked neither silence nor the dark. She had been sixteen before she could be persuaded to sleep without a night-light.

"A canary to whistle. It was a nice idea. Maybe she has gone to find it. Who knows. Come this way, Froken Asherton. The stairs are steep, but it is only two flights."

Willa had never lived anywhere without imprinting her unmistakable mark on a place. It was here, triumphing over the modern utility furniture, the austere polished floors, the severe light fittings. A table lamp with a frilled yellow shade, a dark painting in an enormous gilded antique frame that took up half of one wall, an amusing pot-bellied china stove painted with a floral design, Persian rugs in front of the deep couch, a mass of brilliantly coloured cushions, curtains tied back with velvet bows, pot plants—Willa had always been clever with pot plants—along the

9

windowsill. And the empty birdcage made in the shape of a Chinese pagoda.

Willa had used to say that she had all the instincts of an itinerant junk collector. After only six months in Stockholm she had collected quite an amount of expensive junk. That dark picture looked like an original. The Persian rugs had an authentic rich faded look. How could Willa have bought them on her salary as a secretary at the British Embassy? Had a friend lent them to her, or given them to her?

"It's nice," Grace said, since Fru Lindstrom standing in the doorway obviously expected some comment.

"Yes. She has made it very pretty. Always she was finding something new. You must see her bedroom and her bed."

The bedroom was small, but charming, with the pale grey bed with curved ends, like a baby's cradle, and the pale grey dressing table and wardrobe to match. If the bed were a genuine antique it must have cost a great deal. It was probably a copy but even then not cheap.

"It is Gustav the third," Fru Lindstrom explained, knowledgeably, touching the curved ends.

"Genuine?"

"*Nej*. But even so quite old. It was in a bad state when she brought it here, but Herre Polsen helped her to paint it."

"Herre Polsen?"

"He is the gentleman above. He has the attics and bumps his head." Fru Lindstrom went into her unexpected chuckles. "He is too high in the head."

"He's Swedish?"

"Half Swedish, half Danish. He teaches at the university."

"Perhaps my cousin told him where she was going," Grace said hopefully.

"Perhaps. It was not my business to enquire." The woman rattled the keys in her hand. "Then what plans have you since your cousin is not here to welcome you?"

"I don't know." Grace glanced out of the windows at the already darkening sky. The melancholy that had touched her at the airport when Willa was not there to meet her touched her again. The perplexity, too. Where on earth had Willa gone? "Could I spend the night here?" she asked.

Fru Lindstrom considered.

"I think that could be permitted. I am only the caretaker, but the apartment is your

11

cousin's, the rent is paid. Why not? Who can object? Hotels in this town are very expensive."

"Willa might be back by tomorrow."

"That is so."

"You're quite sure she didn't say how long she would be away?"

" 'A short time', she said. What is a short time? One week, two weeks?"

"How did she seem? Happy? Excited? I mean, as if she were going on a holiday?"

"Just in a great hurry, as if she had a train to catch. I regret I cannot tell you more, Froken Asherton."

"You've been very kind. I will stay here. And I'll telephone the Embassy. They must know where my cousin is. She wouldn't just walk out of her job. She must have had some leave she wanted to take before the winter."

"That is true. The winter is long enough when it begins. The English don't like our winter." Fru Lindstrom gave her sudden smile, her plump face creasing in a dozen jolly creases, but her pale eyes remaining untouched by any expression. "Then I will leave you. If you wish anything, knock on my door, I am always there."

When she was alone in the pretty room the

unease swept over Grace too strongly. The expensive rugs, the dark picture, the bed not a genuine antique, but old, nevertheless . . . What sort of a life was Willa leading? Was someone keeping her? Even if this were so, it was nothing to feel too distressed about. Nothing to make a mystery out of.

Yet there was undeniably something melancholy in the too quiet apartment. The windows looked over the lake, steely grey in the twilight, the bobbing boats tied up, the copper green of the palace roof and church spires on the opposite bank turning black as the light faded. It was a wonderful view. It must be full of colour and sparkle in the summer. But now it was muted, chilly, desolate. Grace drew the curtains to shut it out, and switched on the lamp under the frilly yellow shade.

She tried to think constructively. There would be nothing to eat in the flat. She must go out and shop before the shops closed. But first she must telephone the Embassy and ask to speak to Willa's boss. A man called Sinclair. He was one of the junior diplomats. That much she knew. Willa had written, "My boss, Peter Sinclair, is a very decent chap, he doesn't work me too hard."

"I don't get you. Who did you say you are?"

"Grace Asherton, Willa Bedford's cousin. Isn't Willa your secretary?"

"Was."

The voice was laconic, uncaring. *Was!*

"Isn't she now? I mean, I know she's away at present because I've just arrived to visit her, and found an empty flat. But she'll be back, surely. All her things are here."

"Hold it. One thing at a time. I guess she'll be back for her possessions, but not to her job here. She gave it up, didn't you know?"

Grace's fingers tightened round the telephone. Fru Lindstrom must have switched off the heat in here. It was distinctly chilly.

"No, I didn't know."

"She didn't tell you she was getting married?"

"Married!"

The voice in the telephone became a little dryer. "Obviously she didn't. Well, she gave us a surprise, too."

"But who did she marry? Do you know that?"

"No. Afraid I don't. Some character called Gustav. Look, we can't very well discuss this on the telephone. Come and see me if

14

you're worried, and I'll tell you all I can."

"Are you worried, Mr. Sinclair?"

Did the short dry laugh come too quickly?

"Not in the least. Willa was a fantastic girl, but between you and me, not the most reliable of secretaries."

Was, again. Surely a slip of the tongue.

"I would like to come and see you, Mr. Sinclair."

"Yes, do that. Not here. Come to my flat. My wife would like to meet you. This evening?"

"Could it be? I confess I am worried."

"Sure. Six o'clock? Take a cab. We're in an apartment block just off the Valhallavagen. It's called Vasahuset. Number nine, second floor. Got it?"

"Yes."

"Right. See you then."

And the room was silent again, more silent than ever as Grace looked at the empty birdcage, the drooping pot plants, the narrow grey bed through the open door of the bedroom. A single bed. That didn't mean anything, particularly, except that Willa had probably not had a lover living with her. Anyway, Fru Lindstrom would have been bound to drop an interesting piece of information like that.

Grace went to the kitchen and ran some water into a jug to water the plants. It would be a pity if they were dead when Willa returned, although she should have thought of that.

But what were pot plants compared to a brand new husband?

Was this the situation she hadn't known how to get out of? Was she pregnant? Grace knew that she had already had one abortion, two years ago. She had had it done secretly, and not told Grace about it until it was three weeks' past. But then, white and unhappy, she had confessed that she hated herself for it, she had felt the most enormous guilt. She kept having a dream about a dead baby in her arms.

She said it had been the only thing to do, the man, whoever he was, had wanted no responsibility, and it would have been unfair and crazy to bring such an unwanted child into the world. The cards got stacked against you enough as you grew up, without starting life that way. But she would never do such a thing again.

Willa's resilience had quickly got her over

that brief period of depression, and she had soon plunged into her version of having a good time. That was when she had begun wearing dark glasses to parties, which may or may not have had significance. Only Grace knew what a complex person she was, but even she, in spite of their childhood and the greater part of their teens spent together, and their close blood ties, didn't understand her completely.

"You can be sure I won't be caught again," she had said more than once, about that unhappy episode.

So if she were caught now, it must be because she had wanted to be. Was it the father, the mysterious Gustav, who wasn't so enthusiastic about the situation?

This was all pure speculation. Grace only hoped that Peter Sinclair would be able to clarify matters. How much did a secretary confide in her boss? Depended on the boss. Perhaps Willa had some girl friends in the Embassy, though she had never been one to make close friendships with women. In a foreign country, where they were all exiles, it could be different.

Could it?

Absently, Grace opened her suitcase, and

began to unpack. Expecting a visit of no more than a week, she hadn't brought a lot of things. Wardrobe space should be no problem—except that the wardrobe in Willa's bedroom was literally crammed with Willa's clothes.

Hadn't she taken anything to wear on her honeymoon? Or had she gone mad about clothes, and bought everything new, ignoring that perfectly smashing glittering gold cocktail dress, the fashionable silk jersey culottes, the little red suit that looked brand new, the slacks and jumpers, the shaggy black fur coat (just the thing for the country in this chilly weather), the rows of shoes with hardly a scuffed heel among them.

Was she marrying a millionaire?

With a hand that trembled slightly, Grace began opening the drawers of the dressing table. It was hard to guess how much make-up had gone, Willa had always had dozens of mysterious pots, nor did Grace know about her jewellery, although there were two or three pieces of quite good junk stuff here. Lingerie she couldn't possibly judge. It stood to reason that Willa would have bought a sexy new negligée and nightgown. And the dressing gown hanging behind the door had seen better days.

But the clothes in the wardrobe were definitely puzzling. Had Peter Sinclair or anybody ever seen Willa in that gold cocktail dress? It wasn't exactly standard wear for a shorthand typist at an Embassy party.

"Oh, Willa!" Grace burst out aloud. "Why on earth have you come over so secretive? If you didn't want me to know what you were up to, why did you send me that S.O.S.? Now I suppose I'll find the refrigerator full of food?"

Which was exactly what she did, although it couldn't be said that it was over-stocked. Just the usual basic things such as butter, frozen vegetables, eggs, a half loaf of bread, the remains of a joint carefully wrapped in polythene.

The kind of things one would leave if one were only going to be away a day or two. Or had left too suddenly to attend to details like that.

2

THE door of the flat in Vasahuset was opened by a little girl, freckle-faced, plain, pig-tailed. Behind her stood a little boy, equally plain.

"Hullo," said Grace. "Does Mr. Sinclair live here?"

The children burst into giggles.

"Of course he does. He's our father," said the girl pertly, and the boy, less pert but not to be outdone by his sister, said, "Fathers always live with their mothers and children."

"Be quiet, Alexander! The lady knows that. My brother is only four," the little girl explained to Grace, at the same time adding politely, "Won't you come in?"

A voice shouted from the living room.

"Georgy! Alexander! Don't keep Miss Asherton standing on the doorstep."

"She's coming in, Daddy. I just invited her."

A man appeared, smoothing thick fair hair. He wasn't handsome, his skin was sprinkled with faded freckles (which his children had inherited), he was a little too pudgy, but the smile he gave Grace had charm.

"Miss Asherton? Do come in. These talkative brats are in the process of being taught to be seen but not heard, if you can believe it. We should have begun years ago. Go upstairs, both of you." He held out his hand for Grace's coat. The children were already protesting.

"But Daddy, it's only six o'clock. We haven't had our supper."

"*Upstairs!*" roared their father, pointing.

The children, acknowledging defeat, fled. Peter Sinclair gave a rueful smile, motioning Grace into the living room.

"Not my best diplomatic effort. Those kids are spoilt. My wife says it comes from always living abroad. What will you drink? Sherry, gin, the drink of the country, schnapps. No, you'd better not have that. The Swedes are rather fanatical about only having it with food. And very good it is then."

"I'd love a Scotch," Grace confessed. "I must admit I'm absolutely all at sea. Coming here to see Willa, and finding this mystery."

"Was she expecting you?" Peter Sinclair asked, his back to her as he stood at the cocktail cabinet.

21

"No. I came on the spur of the moment."

"Well, then. No mystery. Willa didn't expect you, therefore wasn't waiting to meet you. Did you say you were her cousin?"

"Yes. But we're more like sisters, actually. We have a very close relationship."

Peter Sinclair had turned to hand her the drink. He looked at her critically.

"You don't look alike. Not in the least."

He was emphatic about that. Grace thought he was dismissing her quieter appearance as uninteresting. So it was, not only in comparison with Willa's tendency to flamboyance, but because she had always been withdrawn with an introspective often scowling face, hair that for all its shaping and brushing usually took on an appearance of untidy spiky ends, a body that was even thinner than Willa's, and small blunt-fingered hands.

"I didn't say we were alike. I merely said we understood each other. Told each other everything. Or most things, I guess."

"But not an important thing like marriage plans," the man said thoughtfully, dropping ice into another glass. "That's what's worrying you?"

"Of course. Wouldn't it you?"

"I suppose it would, if I was as close to somebody as you say you were to Willa. I don't know. In the big things, I find people can be extraordinarily secretive. For fear of opposition to their plans, perhaps."

"Why do you keep saying was? And were?" Grace asked. "You did on the telephone, too. You said Willa was a fantastic girl. Now you're saying I *was* close to her, not that I *am*."

"Good gracious, you are sensitive about small things, aren't you? I didn't mean anything. I suppose I'm already seeing Willa in the past. After all, she's been gone ten days, and I've got a new girl, a Miss Jenkins, fantastic typist. I can't give her enough work. But she intimidates me. I think I preferred your cousin's slapdash methods." He shrugged. "Secretaries come and go. Didn't you know that? You're not one yourself?"

"No."

He was waiting to be told what she was. Grace didn't oblige. She had the feeling that he was deliberately keeping off the subject of Willa's disappearance, cleverly leading her down other trails. This came from being a diplomat, she supposed.

"Please, Mr. Sinclair, tell me about this Gustav. Or whoever he is."

"That's what Willa always called him. And my name's Peter. Let's be friendly. What's yours?"

"Grace. But did you never meet him?"

"No. I was only Willa's boss, you know. I didn't pry into her private life."

"Of course not. I understand that. But knowing what a chatterbox Willa was— and with something as important as being married I'd have thought she would have told you more."

"Isn't that what I just said? The bigger the thing the more secretive a person can be."

"If there's something to hide," Grace said uneasily.

"Such as a runaway marriage?"

"Is that what it was?"

"Looks like it, doesn't it?"

"But why?"

"Who knows? Opposition from the man's family, perhaps. Perhaps he was already married and had to get a divorce. Perhaps he wanted to present everybody with a *fait accompli*."

"Don't you really know anything more than that?"

Peter sat on the sofa beside Grace. He had large very sincere blue eyes that now looked into hers. She imagined him looking in the same way at a recalcitrant secretary, or at a foreigner who failed to understand the British point of view.

"I'll tell you exactly how much I know, which is damn little. Willa was quite a party girl. I expect you knew that. Lately she had been having too many late nights, arriving late to work, and making shocking mistakes. Really, her work was getting to be a mess. I had to tell her off several times. She said she was sorry. She was involved with this character Gustav. He never wanted to go to bed. No, what I meant was that he let her get precious little sleep. I don't know whether they went to bed or not. That wasn't my affair. I was only worried about badly-typed letters, and unpunctuality. It was a pity. We all liked Willa. My wife did, too. She used to come here and babysit for us. Until she met Gustav and then she never had time."

"Gustav is Swedish?"

"Seems so, doesn't it? A name like that."

"But Willa never told you anything about him?"

"No. I have the idea he lived in the

country. Though where I got that from, I don't know. Willa used to go off for weekends. Then one morning two weeks ago she burst into my room, five minutes early for once, and said she was giving notice. She was going to be married. And would it be highly inconvenient if she packed up and left there and then?"

"That very minute!"

"Practically."

"Did you agree?"

"I couldn't do much else. I could see I wouldn't get any sense out of her if she stayed. She knew I could get a temporary girl from the pool. She wasn't interested in another week's wages, or what was owing to her, come to that. She went off without leaving an address, and there's still a cheque waiting for her to collect."

"So actually no one at all knows where she is."

"As of now, no. But don't look so alarmed, Grace. She'll turn up. Have another drink."

Grace let him take her glass. She was trying to think of all the practical things she should ask.

"Tell me this, Mr. Sinclair. I mean Peter. Do you think she was pregnant?"

He was slow in answering. He was lifting ice with silver tongs, dropping it with a plop into the glass.

"That could be," he said at last.

"Are you guessing? Or did she tell you so?"

"No, she didn't tell me. She only made an oblique remark about getting to the altar in time. Not so oblique if you analyse it. I expect her meaning was crystal clear."

"She apparently had several months in which to get to the altar," Grace said dryly. "If she didn't even look pregnant."

"Yes. I think the implication was that Gustav might change his mind. She was catching him in the way she would catch a train."

Peter suddenly began to laugh, his blue eyes merry.

"I don't know why we're being so doom-like. This is surely a happy occasion. Willa has caught the man she wanted. If she hadn't wanted him she wouldn't have let a little mistake like a pregnancy drive her into his arms. Before long she'll turn up, a blooming bride."

"Did he want to be caught, I wonder?" Grace murmured. "Are Swedes honourable about these things?"

27

"As much as most men, I should think. Mind you, if a girl sets out deliberately to trap a man in that way—"

"Willa wouldn't do that," Grace said indignantly. "I know. I know her. But she wouldn't have an abortion, either, to please anybody."

"Why wouldn't she do that?"

"Because she had one once, and it nearly broke her heart. She was guilt-ridden for ages. She said the baby would come back to haunt her."

"Goodness me. That's a side of Willa I didn't know."

"Should you have?" came a voice from the doorway.

They both turned to see the woman standing there, a slight dark-haired person with curiously lacklustre eyes.

"Kate," said Peter, springing up. "Come and meet Grace. Willa's cousin. I told you she was coming. My wife Kate, Grace."

They shook hands. Kate's hand was limp. She looked tired. There were dark circles round her eyes.

"Hullo," she said. "You're not like Willa, are you? How did you happen to come to Stockholm so soon? Did Willa send for you?"

28

"No. Well, not exactly. She wrote me a letter that I didn't understand."

"Goodness, you must be fond of each other if you would fly here because of a mysterious letter."

"She didn't answer my telegram," said Grace. "That isn't like her. And yes, we are close." Her tone was slightly aggressive. Why should this blasé woman think emotion between families strange?

"You didn't tell me about the letter," said Peter.

"I hadn't got around to it. Is it important?"

"Only according to what was in it."

The cry for help? Grace had no intention of telling that secret arrangement to a stranger. At least, not yet. If things got more mysterious or alarming—but they wouldn't, of course. Kate was taking the drink her husband handed her, and drinking it as if she were thirsty. Her dark eyes watched Grace from over the top of the glass.

"There was nothing much in the letter," Grace said. "Willa just said she had got into a situation that she couldn't get out of. I expect it meant, as Peter says, that she was pregnant. Did you think so?" she asked Kate.

"Yes, I did. Since you ask me. Not that she

29

told me so. She kept that confidence for my husband."

Was the flatness of her voice hiding bitterness? But this young woman's attitude was all downbeat, as if nothing pleased or amused her. She was quite a contrast to her husband with his direct persuasive smile.

"You're wrong, love," Peter said easily. "She didn't tell me. She only hinted. But I can put two and two together."

"She nearly passed out here one evening," Kate said. "After only one drink. She said she was tired. Too many late nights. But if you've had a baby yourself you know the look. When she gave her notice the next week, I could put two and two together. Besides, she was suddenly wearing that ostentatious ring."

"Kate means that it looked like a family heirloom," Peter explained. "It was a man's signet ring, actually, lapis lazuli with an engraved coat-of-arms. Willa had to wear it on her middle finger. It was too big for her."

"Would this be the coat-of-arms of Gustav's family?"

"Haven't the slightest clue," Peter said cheerfully. "I'm not up on the old Swedish families. We don't move in those circles. Do we darling?"

"So what do you plan to do, Grace?" Kate asked. "Stay here until Willa turns up?"

"Yes. I do." Grace made the decision, in that moment. "I can stay in her flat. The caretaker is a jolly Swedish lady with eyes like white marbles. She tells me the rent is paid until the end of the year, so of course Willa will be back. Anyway, she's left practically all her things behind. A marvellous Gustav III bed. I can see Stockholm while I wait."

"Enjoy yourself," Kate said ironically.

"Don't you like it? I thought it a very handsome city, from the view I've had from taxi windows."

"Wait until the winter. Wait until it's never daylight, and the snow falls, and the night goes on forever. I've had one winter here and I don't know how I didn't go mad."

Peter put his arm round his wife in an affectionate gesture.

"Kate still hankers for Surbiton, don't you love? You were the same in Cyprus, where there was plenty of sun. It isn't only the great northern winter, it's permanent homesickness."

Kate made a sudden movement, snuggling her head into his shoulder.

Peter looked over her head at Grace.

"I've applied for a home job after my tour here is finished. But I've got another two years, and you'll have to stick it, darling, or have me a junior clerk all my life."

"I absolutely dread the winter," Kate muttered. "The children indoors all the time, the noise they make, and every time you look out of the window it's dark. It gives me the willies."

"Oh, come off it, love, it isn't as bad as that. You get to plenty of parties."

"Embassy parties."

"Well, they're not too bad. Duty free liquor. Plenty of new faces. We have one here right now. Grace, will you come to a small do we're having tomorrow evening? As my wife says, it will be mostly Embassy people, but you'll meet everyone who knew Willa. Someone might be able to tell you something."

"I'd love to come," said Grace. "How nice." She rose to go.

"I'll drive you back," said Peter. "Okay, darling?" He gave his wife another squeeze. "Won't be long. Tell the kids I'll be up to say goodnight."

In the car Peter gave a barely perceptible sigh, and said, "I'm sorry Kate put on her act. I'm afraid she usually does."

"Is she so unhappy here?"

"I suppose she is. It's really more a matter that she won't be happy. She knew this would be our kind of life when she married me. She's a great family girl, is Kate. Wants everyone around, Mum, Dad, aunts, the lot. Especially when it's Christmas or the kids' birthdays. She's unalterably surburban at heart, bless her."

"And you're not?"

"Oh, God!"

"But don't get me wrong," he said, after a pause. "We belong to each other. We take the bad with the good. She stays here another two years, then I do a stint of home duty. But hey, what am I doing, airing my problems, when its yours we're supposed to be sorting out."

"Not mine, Willa's."

"Oh, Willa hasn't any now. Mark my words. What do you do, Grace? For a living, I mean."

"I write."

"Do you now?" His voice was full of admiration. "Books?"

"Novels."

"Ah ha! So that explains your flights of imagination."

"About Willa? But I have only been sorting out facts."

"With a highly melodramatic turn of mind, if I may say so. Flying off to Stockholm like this. Nice for us, though. You're an attractive girl, Grace. Different from Willa."

"Thank you," said Grace, knowing he was the kind of man who thought he had to say flattering things to a girl, knowing also that he didn't mean a word of it. "That isn't exactly the point."

"It's always a point in a girl's life. Don't argue that one. And by the way," he had stopped the car outside the house on Strand-vagen and turned to look seriously at Grace, "don't get it into your head that this could be a matter for the police."

"But I hadn't thought any such thing," Grace exclaimed genuinely shocked.

"I was only thinking—with your novelist's mind—it wouldn't do, you know, we couldn't have a scandal. One's country's prestige and all that. Get me? Goodnight, Grace. Look forward to seeing you tomorrow evening."

3

THE door of the ground floor flat opened an inch as Grace went in. So Fru Lindstrom was one of those irritating people, a listener, a peeper. It was not surprising, considering her interest already in Willa's absence and Grace's arrival. She was probably hoping Grace was going to tap on her door and report on her activities. When Grace, with ostentatiously loud footsteps, began to climb the stairs, the door closed softly, regretfully.

Grace had no time at this moment for Fru Lindstrom. She was seething with indignation. Her novelist's mind, indeed! Was Peter Sinclair mocking her concern for Willa? She hoped he was. She sincerely hoped so. Because if his warning about the police had been made in all seriousness, then it meant that he was afraid she might uncover something disturbing.

Inside Willa's quiet flat, with all the lights switched on for comfort, Grace sat down to think constructively.

Willa had sent her secret S.O.S. She must have known it would bring an immediate response from Grace. But she hadn't waited for the response. She had gone off even before Grace's telegram had arrived. So either she was about to come back, or she had left some message for Grace to find on her arrival.

The flat must hold a clue. Willa was the kind of person who hid things in eccentric but obvious places. Her jewellery in an old teapot, for instance, her diary under her pillow. Grace gave an exclamation, surprised at herself for forgetting the most important clue.

Willa's diary was as much a part of herself as her make-up, her conversation, her individual manner. She imagined herself a twentieth-century Fanny Burney, recording for posterity the life of an average young woman of modern times. It was not to be published until forty years after her death, she said in complete seriousness, which was a pity because Grace already had the pleasure of seeing her own work in print, and that was something to be envied.

"But I am a diarist, not a novelist," Willa sighed. She had occasionally let Grace read some extracts of the precious volumes.

(There were already ten of them locked away in a box among Willa's possessions in England.) The writing was untidy and undisciplined, like her letters, but in places it had a strange power, especially the account she had written of her abortion. Her pain and anguish had started out of the page. To her, the diary was a confessional and an absolution. It somehow enabled her to keep her curious innocence in spite of her impulsive and not always admirable behaviour.

So there must be a current diary in the flat, unless she had taken it with her.

Grace sprang up and began searching, throwing things about in her impatience. Was it hidden behind books on the bookshelf, in the drawers of the writing-desk—no, too obvious—inside cushions that unzipped, under the floor rugs, behind the large dark painting on the wall, among plates in the sideboard, under the pillows or the mattress of the pretty bed, in the wardrobe, in the dirty linen basket in the bathroom, behind tins of sugar and tea in the kitchen cupboard, in the refrigerator.

"I'm afraid it's no use looking in there, Willa never kept enough food to feed a hungry mouse. I have taken the liberty of preparing something, which is here."

The tall man in the doorway was holding a covered tray. In her fright, Grace had dropped the bony joint wrapped in polythene.

"Throw that away, it looks nasty," the man said. "Do you want to get food poisoning? Then we would have another calamity."

"Another?"

"Willa's departure is already one, isn't it?"

"Who are you?"

"Polsen. I live on the top floor."

"Just Polsen?"

"I have a first name, but you would never be able to pronounce it. Now tell me who you are."

His slow ponderous manner was reassuring. Grace relaxed and said, "I'm Grace Asherton, Willa's cousin. I've come to visit her and found her gone. What's under that cloth?"

Polsen whipped the cover off the tray, exposing the arranged dishes.

"Soup. Soused herring. Cheese. Butter. Rye bread. Coffee, schnapps and beer. Okay?"

Grace shut the refrigerator door with a bang. She sighed with pleasure. The diary could wait.

"I'm starving. I hadn't realised."

"So am I. We have enough here for two. May I sit at the table with you? Willa and I did this sometimes. But not often, I am sad to say, for my own sake. She led a very busy life."

Grace sat down, looking with frank interest at her visitor. He was very tall, with untidy dark hair and a long gloomy bloodhound kind of face. He wore a shaggy high-necked pullover over corduroy trousers. His eyes looked myopic behind strong glasses. Grace wondered if he ever smiled. She wondered how much those myopic eyes, with their mild impersonal gaze, really saw. She sighed again with pleasure, not only at the prospect of food, but at having another source of information to investigate.

"Can we eat before I ask you questions?"

"Sure. Questions with coffee? You can tell me about yourself in the meantime."

"I expect Mrs. Lindstrom told you about me?"

"In this house, news flies. You must drink your schnapps with the fish. Soup first."

Grace took a spoonful.

"Delicious."

Polsen nodded his big head solemnly. "Oh,

yes, I am a first-class cook when I have the time. I teach at the university and I paint a little and do a little housework, and ski in the winter and try to read all the books I want to."

"No wife?"

"Not at present."

"What is that supposed to mean?"

The strange eyes behind the thick spectacles looked at her ringless fingers.

"No husband?"

"Not at present," Grace retorted, then frowned at herself. "That was unfair. After you bringing me this lovely meal. No, I haven't got a husband. So far I've spoilt my chances by being married to my typewriter. I've always been much more cautious than Willa. She goes too much one way, I the other."

He spent quite a long time looking at her. He was one of those slow reflective men who pondered immensely before he committed himself to speech.

Then he gave an admiring smile, and said, "That was clever."

"How?"

"You are so honest that courtesy compels me to be honest, too. I have a wife, of course.

After all, I'm nearly forty years old. But we live apart. I have a son whom I see every Sunday. I wouldn't want to lose that privilege. He's a nice little fellow. I'm going to teach him to ski this winter. So that's how it is."

"But if you should fall in love again?"

"Me?" Grace thought his wry look was sad. She wondered what Willa had thought of him. Dull but useful probably. Willa never despised usefulness in people.

"Now the schnapps." He filled two glasses to the brim with the honey-coloured liquid, and lifted his own. "*Skol!*"

Grace imitated his action. She was feeling happier and relaxed. She had needed food, and perhaps this undemanding conversation, too. It had been a long lonely day.

"I'm at least going to enjoy Stockholm, now that I'm here."

"Then you didn't bring your uncomfortable bedfellow?"

"My which?"

"The typewriter you find so inseparable?"

Grace gave a small snort, acknowledging his joke, although it didn't amuse her.

Jokes about lady novelists never did and she feared he was about to make one.

She laid down her knife and fork and deliberately changed the subject.

"Tell me what you know about Willa, Polsen. Did you meet her friends? This Gustav. Did you meet him?"

"Gustav?"

"That's the name of the man she's supposed to be marrying. Hadn't you heard of him?"

"No, I hadn't."

Grace raised her eyebrows in astonishment.

"You mean Willa never mentioned him to you!"

"Well, she may have. She mentioned men a great deal. There could have been a Gustav. It's a common enough name in Sweden."

"Yet you say you and Willa were good friends."

"I thought so." Polsen wrinkled his brow, looking more than ever like a lugubrious bloodhound. "That didn't mean she told me all her secrets, obviously. Besides, we didn't live on each other's doorsteps. I would have evening classes, or she would have dates. I'm not Fru Lindstrom, with my ear to the door."

"I didn't mean—" Grace began, but was interrupted blandly.

"I am quite happy to be cross-examined."

"I didn't mean to do that, either. I'm only so anxious to get any information. The smallest crumbs. For instance, all these expensive things that don't go with a furnished flat."

Polsen stooped to pick up the cushions from the floor.

"Have you been looking for her under the sofa?"

"Don't make a joke of it, please. I was looking for clues. Willa had a habit of hiding things in strange places."

"But you haven't found anything significant?"

"Only this evidence that she was living beyond her means. How could she buy persian rugs, for instance?"

"I thought she had some private income," Polsen admitted. "She said with the long dark winter coming, she must have colour."

"Everyone seems to be neurotic about the winter."

"It depends."

"Then Willa obviously thought she would be spending the winter here. Fru Lindstrom said she intended getting a canary. What made her change her plans so suddenly?"

"I can only suggest that love produces an unpredictable state of mind."

"Now you sound exactly like a professor! Tell me, did you meet any of the men who came here to see Willa?"

"I don't think so many came here. Willa went out. She had plenty of dates. She had a party here just before she dis—, went away. There were so many people I couldn't have told you who anyone was, with certainty. People from the Embassy, mostly."

"No one called Gustav?"

"Not that I can be sure about. It was a great party, though. Willa had her hair yellow for the occasion. We said she should be put in that pretty birdcage in place of the absent canary."

"That sounds like Willa," Grace said. "Her hair has been every colour except green, at one time or another."

"It looked nice. She said she intended keeping it yellow all the winter. It would brighten the landscape. I mean, it *will* brighten the landscape."

Grace stared at him, not speaking, fighting her unreasonable apprehension again. She was suddenly having an uncomfortable picture of Willa with her sunflower head shivering in a landscape of snow and dark forest.

"We had an arrangement," Polsen went

44

on. "She rapped on the ceiling in the kitchen with a broom handle. Two raps, she wanted to talk, because she got broody when she was alone, three, had I anything to eat because she was dying of starvation."

That all rang true. Willa and her games. The secret signature to letters, the way she hid things, the drama of her disappearance.

"The same rules must apply to you while you stay here, Grace."

"Are you playing nanny to us?" Grace asked, and was immediately remorseful, because of the hurt that came into his face. He didn't quite understand what nanny meant. When told, he was no less hurt.

"I didn't think you would be so sensitive, Polsen."

His heavy head hung down self-consciously.

"You can think me a fool," he said at last. "For a man, I am ridiculously sensitive. But I wasn't a nanny, as you express it, to Willa. She had long ago outgrown the need for that sort of person. I was only a friend. She talked too much, but that was good for a silent creature like myself. I liked her. She was mostly happy, I think."

"Only mostly?"

"That's what I said. Sometimes she needed to be cheered up. She would have had a quarrel with a boy friend—"

"*Which* boy friend?"

"How was I to know? But I can guess when a girl is crying over a man."

"Did she tell you she was pregnant?"

He looked shocked, his dark eyes staring through the thick glasses.

"Was she?" he asked, after several moments.

"The Sinclairs seem to think so."

He leaned forward earnestly. "Then what's the fuss, Grace? The sooner she's married the better. There was never a better invention for a baby than a father. Why don't you stop worrying about her? This could explain everything. So enjoy yourself until she comes back with her husband, and it doesn't matter what his name is, Gustav, Jacob, whoever."

"Yes, that's what everyone tells me to do." Grace sighed. "I suppose there's no alternative." (Except to find Willa's diary which she would succeed in doing when Polsen had gone. The diary simply must explain Willa's cry for help.)

She found it at last in the least obvious, yet for Willa the most obvious, place.

There was a false bottom to the birdcage. The diary fitted exactly into the cavity. One could wonder if it was simply for this purpose that Willa had bought the birdcage. The diary had certainly been bought to record her Swedish stay, for it began on the day of her arrival. There were more than fifty pages of close writing, Willa's tight upright script that never lost its neatness even when she was making a comment that required three exclamation marks.

Grace's heart was beating fast with triumph and relief. Now the mystery would be solved. She could hear Willa crying in outrage, "Grace, don't you dare read that! That's only for future generations!" But the circumstances demanded that Willa's privacy could no longer be respected. Grace was compelled to be an eavesdropper on the next century.

Outside a strong wind had begun to blow. It whined against the windows, and a trickle of cold seemed to come into the room. Grace turned up the heat, wondering if it would kill the pot-plants. She hadn't imagined that chill. The gusts of wind shook the windows making the curtains billow slightly. Perhaps tonight the first snow of the winter would fall. It would be a pity if all those fragile yellow leaves were scattered from the birch trees. Then the countryside would indeed be sombre, and the winter dark begun.

It seemed to begin already in this room when Grace had switched off the lights, leaving only the one by the armchair burning. She was shivering a little as she sat down and commenced to read.

TWO HOURS later she closed the book and rubbed her tired eyes. The room was uncomfortably hot now, and the wind seemed to have died. At least it was no longer howling like wolves, which had been one of Willa's expressions. There were many others.

All those dark trees go on forever, and the rain on the roof is driving me mad . . .

That was written at the end of September. What had gone before was equally graphic, equally forlorn, except for occasional snatches of gaiety when Willa described a party she had given for which she had had her hair dyed canary yellow. But the diary, in actual solid facts, told exactly nothing. It might have been written in code. Sentences that began as if they were going to contain vital information ended in mystery.

Went to Gripsholm Castle, saw a portrait of

Gustav IV, told him it was so like him that now I would always call him Gustav . . .

Him. Who? Grace could have wept from frustration.

The description of Fru Lindstrom. *That peeping Thomasina downstairs.* And Polsen. *The giant in the attic with his schnapps, his old potato drink . . .*

Comments about her job at the Embassy. *I wish Peter wouldn't be so mad at me when I make mistakes. He has no patience.* And later, *this place is full of wolves.* But whether that referred to the Embassy was not clear.

There were references to Kate Sinclair and the children. *Kate says I tell them stories that give them nightmares. Can't I talk about anything but dark forests . . .* Then a strange little entry. *"A house with a little gold dragon door-knocker, so unlikely for the unfrivolous Swedes. In the old town, of course."* And then, unexpectedly, *"I hate those melancholy cemeteries with the tall trees."* But she had been intrigued by *"the king with two queens"* although, maddeningly, she had not explained what she referred to. Later there was another royal reference. *"The poor queen kept in the attic."*

After all those unconnected statements, a coherent entry was welcome.

"*The Backes invited me for a weekend. House by lake, dark wall-paper, dark pictures, lace curtains, fug. Papa watches me all the time. Mama very fat, hands like little white pillows. Ulrika doesn't like Sven liking me, she is too possessive. Unhealthy. I see them both in that dark Strindberg house forever . . .*"

Sven. Was he Gustav?

But that entry had been made in August. The ones that followed made no reference to the weekend at the Backes. There was a cryptic "*Gustav doesn't like my new hair colour, says it makes me too conspicuous.*" But obviously she hadn't changed it for him.

There was a comment on the endless dark red and mustard-coloured houses. "*When I get my own I am going to paint it pink.*"

Then "*Axel with his staring eyes*" and "*Jacob, don't underestimate. These quiet men . . .*"

The last entry but one was "*I should have got that canary, this place is too damn quiet,* and the last one of all, made exactly two weeks ago, said cryptically. "*Almost time to leave. I hope it doesn't snow. Otherwise when will we ever get back?*"

50

4

GRACE caught Polsen before he left for the university. She heard him coming down the stairs and in the manner of Fru Lindstrom waylaid him.

"Can you spare a minute, Polsen?"

He looked at her in his serious thoughtful way.

"Of course."

"I made a discovery last night."

His eyes glinted behind the thick glasses.

"Yes. What was that?"

"I found Willa's diary."

"A diary! It tells you everything?"

Was he more interested than he should be, if Willa had been no more than a casual friend?

"It tells me nothing. It's practically written in code."

"But it's reassuring? It's innocent?"

Grace shook her head miserably. "I hardly slept all night. I might be imagining things again, but I'm sure I'm not. I know Willa too well. She was living in a nightmare, Polsen."

51

"Impossible!"

"Perhaps she didn't show it. Perhaps she only gave way to it when she wrote her diary. She has always used her diary as a confessional. But this time she couldn't even do that because she was too frightened to put things down clearly."

"Grace, you must let me see this diary."

His voice had enough urgency to make her ask, "Why are you so interested?"

Her took her arm, hurting her with the grip of his large hand.

"Will you do me the favour of not looking at me with that suspicion? I was Willa's friend. If she's in trouble, I want to help, just as much as you do. If you want to reject my help, then goodbye! Goodbye!"

He began to go down the stairs, and it was Grace's turn to seize his arm. She couldn't bear to be alone, she found. And it was ridiculous to suspect this nice bear-like man with his ponderous speech and quickly-hurt eyes.

"You wouldn't have time to read it now. You have to go to work."

"Let me take it with me."

Grace only hesitated for a moment. A decision now, and Polsen was her friend. He had

52

been Willa's friend, and Willa had disappeared.

She dismissed the disquieting thought immediately.

"All right. When will you be back?"

"Not until this evening, I'm sorry."

"I have to go to a party at the Sinclairs."

"Then don't stay too long. Come home and we'll talk."

Grace nodded, feeling more light-hearted. The night had been awful, endless and full of half-dreams, and the fancy that she could hear wolves howling. The miraculously radiant pink, windless dawn over a still city had only made her shiver at the window. That warm glowing pink in the sky was false. In reality, it was as cold as ice.

"And, Grace. Listen, but don't talk too much at the party."

"You're not going to warn me about Embassy scandals?"

"Have you been warned already?"

She nodded again. "I suppose Peter Sinclair had to do that. It is important. But everyone is sure to be talking about Willa when they know I'm her cousin."

"Then just listen to what they say."

THE ROOM seemed to be very full of people when Grace arrived. Peter Sinclair saw her and came towards her, giving her the quick attractive smile that made his otherwise ordinary face unexpectedly appealing. "Hullo, Grace, I'm glad you made it. Come and meet some people."

He performed introductions swiftly and efficiently. Grace noticed that he laid emphasis on her success as a novelist, and failed completely to mention that she was Willa's cousin.

"We'll have to find her a Swedish publisher," he said blithely. "Good for British exports."

The names in Willa's diary. Grace had learned them off by heart. Sven, Jacob, Axel, Gustav. Those were Swedish names, and most of the people here were English or American. They were all talking the conversation of exiles.

"You here on a visit, Miss Asherton? Getting copy? You won't want to linger once the winter starts."

"Why not?" Grace asked.

"Well, it's so bloody dark, for one thing. I don't go for perpetual night."

"Are you going to study the Swedish

54

temperament?" someone else asked. "All that Strindberg gloom?"

"In the summer we can get out to our lakeside cottages, but in the winter we absolutely die of boredom."

"Where are you staying, Miss Asherton?"

"In an apartment on Strandvagen."

"You're lucky. Did someone lend it to you?"

"Yes, my cousin, Willa Bedford."

"Willa!"

A middle-aged woman with a plump, over-made-up, too vivacious face stood in front of Grace.

"Did you say you were Willa's cousin? Why ever didn't Peter tell us? Then you can solve the mystery about her."

"What mystery?" Grace asked coolly.

"Isn't there one, after all?" The woman made a moue. "How disappointing! I know Peter said there was none, but we all thought he was covering up. You know, avoiding a scandal. Typist missing from British Embassy sort of thing. are you telling me she really has been married?"

"I didn't say so," Grace said cautiously. "I've only just arrived and I don't know much more than you do. But Willa always was impulsive and unpredictable. I don't really find a situation like this surprising."

"She didn't leave you a note of explanation?"

"She didn't know I was coming."

"Oh!" The woman really was disappointed. The avid light of gossip went out of her eyes. "I'm Winifred Wright," she said. "Passport section. Willa shared mine and Nancy Price's flat when she first came. Then she moved into her own. To tell the truth we were relieved. She was too gay for us old fogeys."

"Too many boy friends?" Grace asked casually.

"Too many late nights. We got tired of lights being switched on in the small hours."

"Sounds like Willa."

"Not that we didn't like her. And I think she liked us, too, because I must say she never looked particularly happy after she started living on her own. Always seemed anxious."

"As if she couldn't pay the rent?"

"Oh, no, not that sort of worry. Boy friend trouble, Nancy thought. Personally I thought she was involved with a married man and that's why she wanted a flat of her own."

"Did you know who this man was?"

"No." Again Miss Wright looked regretful, deprived of a salacious talking point. "There were some rumours that he belonged to an old Swedish family. But now she's got herself married—*if* she has—we'll soon know all about it, won't we?"

"Now, Winifred! What gossip are you telling Grace?" said Kate Sinclair behind them. "Grace, you must take Winifred's stories with several grains of salt. She has the greatest gift for embroidering dull facts. Haven't you, dear?"

Winifred gave a perfunctory smile. She couldn't be rude to her hostess.

"These aren't exactly dull facts, Kate. We were talking about Willa."

"Oh, that girl again."

"Her worried look was because, apparently, she was pregnant," Grace said deliberately. "But now, as you say, she's sorted all that out, so what are we worrying about?"

"What, indeed?" Kate said with such intensity that Grace looked at her in surprise.

She quickly collected herself.

"It's only that I'm sick and tired of the subject of your cousin, Grace. She's not very popular around here. She upset the children and left Peter in the lurch, going off like that.

Winifred, do help me with the drinks. Peter, as usual, is forgetting he isn't supposed to be enjoying his own party. Will you excuse us, Grace?"

A hot small hand slid into Grace's and held it hard.

"Miss Asherton, my brother and I know where Willa is."

Grace looked down at the upturned earnest freckled visage of Georgy Sinclair. The child was dressed in a pale blue party dress that didn't do much for her plainness. Her ginger hair hung lankly to her shoulders. Her eyes were full of a deadly seriousness, dismissing any idea that she might have been joking.

"Where?" Grace asked.

"In the forest."

"*What* forest?"

"Where the elks are. Will you come upstairs and talk to us?"

"Where's Alexander?"

"Upstairs. He's too young for grown-up parties. And I'm not supposed to be here unless I make intelligent conversation."

"Then let's go," Grace said.

ALEXANDER WAS dressed in brilliantly striped pyjamas. His sandy hair (both children had unfortunate colouring) fell in his eyes. All the bedroom windows were closed and the room was in a warm fug. Grace sat on the edge of one of the beds and said, "Well, then. What did Willa used to do? Read you stories?"

"No, she made them up," Georgy said.

"She told us about shooting elks," Alexander added. "I was scared."

"Because you're a baby," his sister said scathingly. "It was only made up. They don't scream like that. Daddy said so. Willa was pretending. She was always pretending."

"About what other things?"

"When she said if she didn't come back one day we was to tell the police," Alexander burst out, wriggling on his pillow.

"No, it wasn't the police, it was the ambassador," Georgy contradicted.

"It was not, Georgy. You don't tell the truf. It was the police. Except that we can't speak Swedish," Alexander added uncertainly.

"Well, there you are, silly."

"And did you tell the police or the ambassador?" Grace asked in a still voice.

Two startled pairs of eyes looked at her.

"I mean, Willa hasn't come back, has she?"

"No, but it's all right 'cause she's got

married," Georgy declared triumphantly. "That's not being stamped on by an old elk. That's not being lost in the forest."

"Is it?" Alexander said appealingly.

The door opened and Peter Sinclair came into the room. He looked annoyed.

"Grace, have these rascals got you under their thumb already? Georgy! Alexander! You ought to know better."

"I liked it," said Grace. "I like children."

"That's all very well, but at a party—"

"Peter!"

That was Kate's voice. It came nearer, urgently. "Peter, Ebba is here. You must come down."

For the briefest moment an unguarded harassed look showed in Peter's eyes. Then he said, "Good gracious! Yes! I didn't think she was coming. Grace, you must come down and meet the Baroness von Sturpe."

A few moments later Grace listened to him saying, "Ebba, may I present Grace Asherton, just arrived from London."

Grace looked at the long pale face made longer by the high coronet of palest blonde hair. She let her hand be taken by the thin cool one. So this was what the Swedish aristocracy looked like, cool, remote, decidedly anaemic with that colourless skin and shining pale blue eyes. But impressive in the simple black dress, with that elongated neck and straight slim body. A little intimidating . . .

"Are you a new Embassy secretary, Miss Asherton?"

There was no use in trying out her shock tactics of announcing that she was Willa's cousin. This woman was too poised to show unguarded reactions.

"No, I'm a writer."

"But how interesting. Are you going to show her about, Peter? She must see the country properly. Perhaps my husband and I can do something. Would you like to see our house, Miss Asherton? It isn't very large or very grand but it's quite old, and typically Swedish."

"How kind," Grace murmured.

"Ebba is the kindest person in Sweden," Peter said enthusiastically. "Aren't you, Ebba? I'm so sorry Jacob couldn't come. Now let me get you two girls drinks."

Kate moved in the background, a small eclipsed figure in her dark dress. When she lifted her eyes Grace caught a look of strain, almost of panic.

Those dull Embassy parties, she had said.

61

But this one, surely, wasn't dull if it could bring that look to her eyes . . .

"Jacob," Grace said to Polsen later that evening. "One of the names in Willa's diary. I know who he is. The Baron von Sturpe. He wasn't at the party, but his wife was. She was very grand. Threw the Sinclairs into a bit of a tizzy. She wasn't the sort of friend you would imagine them having. The ambassador might have known her, but not a junior diplomat. Does the name mean anything to you?"

"Certainly it does. A slightly impoverished, but very old Swedish family."

"Have you met him or the baroness?"

"What would a poor professor be doing in those circles?"

Was that an evasion?

Polsen was making a note in a little book.

"What are you writing down?"

"Jacob—Baron von Sturpe. We must be systematic. But I think we can decide he has had nothing to do with Willa's marriage plans. He is very completely married, I believe, to his beautiful wife. What about the others? Did you meet a Sven, or an Axel?"

Grace shook her head.

"Not even a Gustav?"

"How could I meet Gustav if he's Willa's

bridegroom?" But Grace went on to relate Winifred Wright's theory about Willa being involved with a married man, and the children's fantasy about her being lost in the forest. Polsen made more notes.

"One will have to be as fanciful as the children if one is to understand this extra-ordinarily fascinating document of Willa's. The forest with the rain dripping down. I wonder if the children do know something?"

"Making guesses is all very well," Grace said impatiently. "But can't we do something? If Willa is in some forest cottage can't we find it?"

"Do you know how many thousand of kilometres of forest there are in Sweden?"

"No, but narrowing that down to the clues in the diary—"

"Such as?"

"I suppose the forest ones aren't very clear," Grace said unhappily.

"No. It rains over a wide area. You must make an opportunity to ask the Sinclair children more questions."

Grace nodded. "I'll do that."

"And in the meantime, tomorrow, since it is Saturday and I don't require to work, we'll drive to Gripsholm to see the portrait of Gustav IV."

"That's a wonderful idea."

"I thought so myself."

"You intend to follow all the obvious clues in the diary?"

"We do, together."

"Do you think this will lead us to Gustav?"

"I hope so. Eventually. At least tomorrow we will see what he looks like. I have only an old Volvo, I'm afraid. But we might take a picnic. It's pretty by the lake."

"What fun."

The room was cosy, Polsen's large calm figure reassuring. It was much nicer here than at the Sinclair's party. Grace said so, and saw a look of pleasure on Polsen's face.

"Then would you take off that little Knightsbridge dress and put on something less elegant. You make me feel extremely shabby."

Grace went into Willa's bedroom, laughing.

"What do you know about little Knightsbridge dresses?"

"I've been to London. I'm quite a travelled old fellow."

"If you want to talk about someone elegant you should have seen the Baroness."

"I have no wish to see her. She doesn't sound my kind of woman."

"What is your kind of woman, Polsen?"

"You're laughing at me. What did you have to drink at the party? Schnapps?"

"No, ordinary English gin."

"Tomorrow," said Polsen, "We will take champagne."

Grace put her head round the door.

"What are we celebrating?"

"Willa's marriage, let us hope."

The brief gaiety died.

"But you don't believe in it, do you, Polsen?"

He shook his head slowly.

"A baby, yes. A marriage, no."

"But if she wanted to go somewhere quietly to wait for her baby she would have come to England."

"You mustn't forget Willa's romantic nature, Grace. I think probably she couldn't leave her lover."

"Oh, my God! But you think he's going to leave her? Then surely she would come back here."

"We will see."

"I wonder why the baby isn't mentioned in the diary."

"Perhaps it is, and we've missed it. She hasn't exactly expressed anything very clearly, has she?"

"Not the ring," Grace mused. "She was supposed to be wearing a lapis lazuli ring with a crest. She'd love a present like that, but she doesn't mention it. Do you know, Polsen, I think there's a lot more to all this than a lover and a baby."

She waited for Polsen to disagree, wishing that he would. But he didn't. He said nothing, and the chilly outside air seemed to have invaded the room again.

5

THE fascinatingly strange red brick castle with its round towers, and steep narrow winding stairs pleased Grace enormously. She felt less happy when she stood in front of the portrait of Gustav IV.

Those prominent pale blue eyes, the pink cheeks, the sensuous petulant mouth, the powdered wig and the slight effeminate figure . . . Grace was surprised and repelled and full of uneasiness. Did Willa's lover really look like that? If he had, how could she have been foolish enough to trust him, much less have loved him!

"But he's not even handsome! He doesn't look Willa's type at all."

Polsen studied the portrait from every angle.

"Here you have a bad painting," he pronounced. "It's flat and dead. You must imagine the eyes alive and sparkling and a mile of the lips. It's a feminine mouth, isn't it? It could look pretty, smiling. It could be a quite persuasive face. Personality is always more arresting than good looks." He waved his hand at the painted figure. "You must add the magnetism of warm blood and vitality."

Grace was still doubtful and puzzled. She didn't think that a mouth which looked pretty when smiling was an attribute in a man to be particularly admired.

"Is it a typical Swedish face?" she asked.

"No. I wouldn't say very typical."

"Then if we meet it we should be able to recognise it without difficulty."

"Allowing for modern dress, hair its natural colour, and the animation I spoke of."

"Species, a king of Sweden, circa 1778-1837. You're giving a lecture, Polsen. So we look for someone like this with a strong personality. It will be difficult."

He took her hand. She was surprised at the way her own disappeared within it. His hands and feet were proportionate to the size of his body. She rather liked the way he towered above her.

"Now if we were looking for someone like you, Polsen, you would stand out in a crowd."

"Is that meant to be a flattering remark? I somehow doubt it. But finding Gustav might not be as hopeless as you think. Shall we see all of the castle while we're here? You must think of all the kings' and queens' feet which have climbed these stairs through the centuries."

"Including more recently Willa's and her Gustav's? I wonder if he was promising her the things kings promise queens."

"A promise is one thing. What the lady eventually gets is another." Grace didn't know whether Polsen was referring to unfortunate medieval queens, or to Willa, but his face had its sudden lugubrious look, as if the pampered face in the portrait had made him uneasy, too. And Grace didn't care for the steely glimpses of lake water through the embrasured windows. The lake curled its cold tentacles everywhere, from Stockholm right down to this remote place. In winter its icy grip must be paralysing.

She was letting herself get like Kate Sinclair, neurotic about the coming winter . . .

"BUT DIDN'T you like the little theatre?" Polsen asked later. "Or the paintings of the horses in the attics?"

"Yes. Yes, I did, very much."

"Then stop looking as if you've just escaped from prison."

They were out in the thin sunlight, walking round the edge of the lake. A swan swam slowly among the rusty reeds, a row of yellow and red houses on the far side were reflected in the water, like a slow-burning fire. Crows cawed in the trees. The air was so still that not one of the papery dehydrated leaves fell to the ground.

"Do I?" said Grace. "But you must have realised by now that I have a morbid imagination."

"And what did this morbid imagination tell you?"

"Only that, if Willa's Gustav looks like his predecessor in the portrait, wherever Willa has gone must have been against her wishes."

"Let us open the champagne," said Polsen.

Grace smiled reluctantly. "Very well, I promise to stop brooding."

"Picnics are meant to be enjoyed," Polsen said in his pedantic way.

"I'm not a gay person like Willa. You must have seen that."

"Yes. I've noticed."

Polsen took the hamper out of the back of the car, and spread a rug on the ground. In a thoroughly expert manner he eased the cork out of the bottle of champagne, filled two mugs, and handed one to Grace.

"You think too much," he said. "So do I. That's why my wife left me. I was too dull for her."

"I'm sorry, Polsen. Did it hurt?"

"Of course. Rejection isn't pleasant, no matter what the circumstances. And there's the boy. Have you been in love, Grace?"

"Of course."

"Deeply?"

"I thought so at the time."

"How many times?"

"Only twice." Her voice got the aggressiveness she could never overcome when speaking about her private feelings. "I told you, my typewriter always came between me and other people. I would suddenly have a compulsion to work until two in the morning, and then I would be exhausted. Which isn't good for love. And anyway—"

"Anyway what?"

She held her chin in the air.

"I was the one in both these affairs to feel the most."

"But not enough to put away your typewriter?"

"You must understand I couldn't," she cried. "That's part of me. Without it I'm only half a person."

He studied her in his customary thoughtful way.

"What are your books about, Grace?"

"Oh—young married couples, social problems, the unwanted child, the complications of human nature—you know the kind of thing. It's important."

"Yes, it's important. And so you forget to smile."

"Do I?"

Grace lifted her face with such instinctive anxiety that Polsen bent and kissed her. She was so startled that at first she sat quite still, thinking that the coolness of his lips against hers was pleasant, like the coolness of the champagne. Then she drew back sharply, scowling.

"Why did you do that?"

"Because it seemed to be a nice thing to do."

"For you or for me?"

He began to laugh and his eyes looked less myopic, sharper and clearer, as if he could see very well when he wanted to.

"Really, Grace, you are like those savage

plants that grow in Scotland. All prickles."

"Scotch thistles?" she said, not amused.

"That's it." His big hand fell heavily on her shoulder. "Come and have some food. Sandwiches, chicken, boiled eggs. I hope you're hungry. And if you're going to ask me, did I kiss Willa on picnics, the answer is no."

Grace looked at the ground. She hadn't known he had taken Willa on picnics. It must have been in the summer when it was hot and they could swim.

"We used to bring Magnus along with us," Polsen said, reading her thoughts.

"Magnus?"

"My boy. We were teaching him to swim. Willa swims like a fish. I am like a whale. But it was fun."

"Didn't she go for picnics with Gustav?"

"This was early in the summer. Later she used to go away for weekends."

"Did she tell you where?"

"Occasionally she said she was going with the Sinclairs. They have a cottage in the forest. I imagined that was where she always went."

"So that's why the children talked about the elks in the forest. But she must have gone somewhere else some of the time."

"Yes. I know that, now."

"There's Sven and Ulrika in the Strindberg house."

"True. We have to find out about them. We have plenty to do. Why did you shiver? Are you cold?"

"A goose walking over my grave."

"Come and sit closer to me. Have some more champagne and tell me why you and Willa are so different."

"Why shouldn't we be? We're not sisters, we're only cousins, even if our mothers were twins. Our fathers were very different from each other. Actually, Willa's parents separated when she was quite small. I think all that talkativeness and gaiety of hers is partly an act, compensating for having been deserted by her father. She began to be an awful show-off when she was quite small. My parents were comparatively happy. My mother died soon after Willa's, both of them from the same thing, a heart defect. Isn't it odd, as if they'd shared the same heart! But my father's still alive and I'm devoted to him."

"He takes your work seriously?"

"Oh, yes, indeed. He expects a great deal more of me than I've already done."

"So. That makes it clear. You and Willa have a father complex."

Grace pouted. "Polsen, for a Swede, your English is too good."

"But my analysis?"

"I suppose I have to agree with that, to a point. Willa and I always knew our mothers cared more about each other than about us. That made us grow close. We feel the deepest responsibility for each other."

"I've gathered as much."

"Does that make you understand Willa better?"

"It explains why she does hare-brained things, but not where she is."

Grace raised troubled eyes. "Gustav is hardly a father figure, is he? Not from that portrait. Polsen, I don't think we should be sitting here wasting time drinking champagne."

She caught his look and scowled again.

"I suppose you're going to tell me that Willa would never have said that."

"You're perfectly right. Let alone the insult to a noble wine. Willa was much too greedy to think like that. Perhaps her greediness is the reason for whatever has happened to her now."

He didn't enlarge on that theory, and Grace didn't pursue it. She was afraid he meant the persian rugs and all the other luxuries in the flat. Eventually she supposed they would find out how Willa had acquired them. But not now. The twilight was growing already, and the lake, the castle, the trees, with their ragged leaves had become too forlorn. Grace suddenly wanted to be back in the warmth of Willa's flat, in spite of its perplexing possessions.

What she didn't expect was the strong perfume that assailed her senses when she unlocked the door of the flat two hours later. Willa's perfume, surely! Willa must be home!

But the flat was in darkness.

She switched on the light, calling excitedly, "Willa!"

There was no answer. The living room and the bedroom were empty. Everything was in order. If Willa had dashed in and gone out again, leaving this strong trail of perfume, she would have left things scattered about.

But there were no flung-off clothes, no disorder.

Completely baffled, Grace sat at the dressing table. The scent was strongest here. She could even put a name to it. Balenciaga's

Quadrille. She opened a drawer at random and saw the spilled bottle.

She knew absolutely that she hadn't spilled it. She hadn't touched anything in that drawer. Yet there the bottle lay on its side, the heady scent seeped out from under the loosened stopper.

There was only one explanation. Someone else had looked in this drawer. Today, while she was out.

Fru Lindstrom, of course. Polsen, who had followed her up the stairs after parking the car, listened to her excited exclamations.

"Polsen, we'll have to speak to her. She can't come in here snooping while I'm out. What would she be snooping for?"

Polsen sniffed, wrinkling his nose with distaste.

"That smell is too much of a good thing, isn't it? Very well, come down and ask some questions."

"It must have been her! Don't you agree?"

"I said, ask some questions. Isn't it your English law that a person is innocent until proved guilty?"

"Fru Lindstrom isn't innocent," Grace said dourly. "I've never trusted her from the start."

Fru Lindstrom was dressed in outdoor clothes when she answered their knock. A shaggy fur hat was pulled well down over her ears, as if winter winds were already blowing round street corners. Her cheeks were bright from exercise, her china-doll eyes prominent as she suspected drama.

"Froken Asherton! Herre Polsen! What can I do for you?"

Grace spoke first, in her agitation.

"Someone has been in my cousin's flat. Who did you give the key to?"

The friendliness went out of Fru Lindstrom's face. Her mouth tightened.

"I will tell you, Froken Asherton, that I am not in the habit of handing out keys to strangers."

"Perhaps this person was not a stranger?" Polsen suggested mildly.

This remark made Fru Lindstrom bristle with indignation.

"Herre Polsen, I am surprised at you. A stranger or a friend, I would not give the key. Besides, I have seen no one. On Saturdays I go to my married daughter's. I have just returned, as you can see. I haven't had time even to take off my hat and coat."

She certainly seemed to be speaking the

truth. Her curiosity was rapidly getting the better of her indignation, however, for she couldn't resist asking, "What has happened? Have things been stolen?"

Grace shook her head.

"No, I don't think anything's missing."

"Then how do you know there has been an intruder?"

"A bottle of scent has been spilt. Someone has been going through drawers."

"There are other things in disorder?"

"No-o," Grace said, although now she believed the cushions had been moved, and plumped up too carefully, one of the rugs left slightly askew. It was a mind's eyes picture induced by her uneasiness.

Fru Lindstrom gave her abrupt and disconcertingly hearty laugh.

"Is that all you have to report? A bottle upset. But I expect you did it yourself without noticing. Don't you think so, Herre Polsen? A burglar would leave great disorder."

"Not a burglar," Polsen said in his reflective way. "Someone who was looking for some specific object. Someone who obviously had his own key, since you didn't give him one."

Fru Lindstrom pressed her hands to her ample breast.

"Ah! Now I understand. One of Froken Bedford's boy friends. Some small souvenir that had to be removed. Letters, perhaps." She laughed again, enchanted with her powers of deduction.

"There, you see, you clever people worry about burglars and I think of something quite simple. The unhappy end to a love affair."

"I must say I don't think it very simple that someone has a key which he can use at any time of the day or night," Grace exclaimed.

"Now don't be unhappy, Froken. No one enters this house without my knowing."

"But if you're away, as you were today?"

"Yes, that's true. Then I suppose the lock must be changed to stop these intruders. All the same I am still not convinced. It is easy to upset a small bottle without noticing. Don't you think you did it yourself?"

"Not with that scent," Grace said. "I'd have known at once. The place smells like a perfume factory."

"So the lock must be changed," Polsen said.

"And If Froken Bedford returns and finds her key won't open the door?"

"I'll be here," said Grace.

"And she will be happy about our sensible precautions," said Polsen amiably.

Fru Lindstrom's gleeful laughter broke out again.

"I understand your meaning. If she has a new husband, as you say, Froken Bedford will no longer care for an uninvited visitor."

"How dare she insinuate that Willa lived such an untidy life," Grace said indignantly as they returned upstairs. "She laughs, but her eyes look malicious. She feeds on other people's indiscretions."

"But I remember that she does visit her daughter on Saturdays," Polsen said.

"And whoever came must have known that? And also that we were going to be away all day? Polsen, we must be being watched!"

When he made no denial, as Grace hoped he would, she began to shiver. "I've got to have that lock changed. Who would Willa have been so silly as to give a key to? It can't have been Gustav since obviously she's with him. An earlier boy friend, do you think? Someone who doesn't want it known that he ever came here? Winifred Wright's married man, perhaps?"

Polsen looked wholly admiring.

"Your powers of reasoning are becoming formidable, Grace."

"Willa's diary!" Grace exclaimed. "He knew about it and was afraid he was mentioned in it. He didn't want me, or anyone else, reading it. But he couldn't find it, because I have it here, in my handbag. So he must be Sven or Axel or Jacob. Do you think he's Jacob, the Baron von Sturpe? A prominent man like that wouldn't want a scandal."

"Neither do I see him doing a grubby thing like searching a girl's room," said Polsen. All the same his eyes had their strange glint again, as if some theory were being tested in his brain. It was not one, however, that he intended to discuss with Grace. For all he added was, "You can feel safe tonight. I'm quite sure your visitor won't return. If you are alarmed, don't hesitate to use the broom."

Which remark reduced the slightly sinister situation to comedy. As probably Polsen had intended it should.

"I mean you to use it on the ceiling, not on your uninvited guest, of course. Although it might be best if you did both things."

The telephone rang when Grace was in her bath. The sound was so unexpected that she leapt out and ran dripping across the polished

82

floor of the living room, forgetting even to snatch up a towel. She had been lying in the warm water thinking that the only other tenants in the house, the two old ladies on the first floor, ought to be questioned. They may have seen someone go up the stairs that afternoon, or heard movements overhead.

Two elderly sisters, unmarried, Fru Lindstrom had described them. Quite untroublesome people who kept to themselves and never made complaints.

Two women living a dull stay-at-home life sometimes saw and heard a great deal more than they ever acknowledged.

Now, however, the imperative ringing of the telephone might solve everything. There might be no need to ask questions of the Misses Morgensson, or of anyone else.

For this, Grace's excited blood told her, must be Willa.

"Hullo," she said breathlessly into the receiver.

"Grace? This is Kate Sinclair."

"Oh, Kate." The anti-climax was too disappointing. (But why had she imagined that Willa would telephone to what should be an empty flat?)

"You sound upset."

"No, It's just that I'm dripping from my bath. Will you hold on a minute while I get a towel?"

When she came back swathed in one of Willa's large bath towels she was calm again.

"How are you, Kate? And the children?"

"Fine. Peter asked me to ring. He thought you might be lonely."

"No, I'm not lonely. I've spent the day sightseeing. We went to Gripsholm Castle and had a picnic."

"Isn't it a bit chilly for picnics? Just a minute." There was some murmuring and Kate went on, "That was Peter. He wants to know who you went with."

"Is that any of his business?" Grace said lightly. "As a matter of fact it was my neighbour. Or Willa's neighbour. A very large kind Swede called Polsen who lectures at the university. He gave me a private lecture today on the portraits at Gripsholm."

There was some more murmuring in the background, then Kate's voice came again, "I'm sorry, Grace. Peter just wants me to explain to you that it *is* his business to see that British tourists don't get into trouble."

"Then he does think Willa's in trouble!" Grace exclaimed.

There was the sound of an indrawn breath, then Peter Sinclair's pleasant crisp voice came through.

"That's exactly what I'm getting at, Grace. Don't be like Willa, running around with men you know nothing about."

"For goodness sake! I couldn't be more different from Willa. And you must know Polsen."

"I've met him, yes. Don't know much about him. And neither do you. But I'm not giving you a lecture. Kate and I only wondered how you were getting on, and whether you would like to come with us tomorrow. We're driving out to our country cottage for the day. It's really too late in the year, but we like to get out of town. You could see something of the country."

The forest where Willa was lost, as the children had told her, their eyes large and strained.

Grace said without hesitation, "I'd love to. Thanks for asking me."

"Splendid. We'll pick you up about ten. Okay? Wrap up well. It'll be cold. I'm taking my gun, I might get a shot at an elk."

GRACE DRESSED quickly, thinking that things were at least happening, even if none of them proved anything. Now she intended paying a call on the Misses Morgensson to introduce herself as their temporary neighbour, and to ask them if they had heard any suspicious sounds overhead that afternoon. The Balenciaga perfume still hung in the air, constantly reminding her of Willa's absence, and of the expensive tastes she had acquired. Why hadn't she taken the bottle of perfume with her, for instance? That was not too unreasonable a question to want answered.

A white-haired old lady opened the door of the flat on the first floor, and peered at Grace with red-rimmed watery eyes.

"Do you speak English?" Grace asked, and the old lady tilted her head on one side, like an alert but slightly deaf white-crested cockatoo.

"Eh? English? *Ja, ja.*"

Grace raised her voice. "I'm Grace Asherton, Willa Bedford's cousin. I'm staying upstairs."

"With Froken Bedford? How nice. Won't you come in and meet my sister? But don't waste your time trying to talk to her. She is quite deaf. She understands no one but me."

Miss Morgensson hadn't boasted when she said she could speak English. Her pronunciation was as perfect as her manners. She took Grace into the cosy living room with its lamps and plush table cloths and embroidered antimacassers, and indicated an exactly similar old lady who sat in a rocking chair rocking gently, her eyes closed.

"Katerina!" she said loudly. "Wake up! We have a guest."

Another pair of vague watery eyes rested on Grace.

"Eh? Who is the young lady?"

The sister shouted again. "Froken Bedford's cousin, from England. Isn't that nice? This is my sister Katerina, Miss Asherton. I am Anna. You will sit down and have some coffee with us, won't you? Don't say you haven't time because it is already hot. Katerina, Miss Asherton is going to stay and have some coffee."

Katerina rocked and smiled and stared. She wore a grey dress with an old-fashioned high neck, her sister an exactly similar style in brown. They both looked pink-cheeked, healthy and cheerful. If spinsterhood could bring them to this comfortable contented old age there was something to be said for it.

Better than Willa, run ragged with her tortuous affairs. Or Grace with hers, for that matter. Except that her wounds didn't show in any way but the now permanently sober aspect she took of life.

"My sister has been deaf for a long time," Miss Anna explained, bustling about with coffee cups.

"Then it's no use asking her if she heard anything unusual this afternoon," Grace said, "Did you, Miss Anna?"

"Unusual!" The old lady paused, her head tilted in that listening look.

"I was out all day and I think someone came into my flat."

"A burglar! *Nej!*"

"No, not a burglar." She was sorry for the alarm she had put in this kindly creature's face. "Just one of Willa's friends, I expect. I only wondered if you had seen anyone go upstairs."

"No, we saw nobody. My sister and I always take a nap after our midday meal. In any case, with no offence meant, we had learned not to notice the number of people going up the stairs since Froken Bedford lived in the flat above. She was young, we said. She had her life to live. But now the child has gone off, we are told. So suddenly! What Axel will say we can't imagine. Can we, Katerina?"

The rocking chair stopped.

"What did you say, Anna? Speak more clearly."

"I said how disappointed Axel would be when he returned to find Froken Bedford gone."

"Axel?" said Grace, her heart beating fast. (Jacob, Sven, Axel, Gustav . . .)

"Our nephew."

"He lives with you?"

"Oh, dear, no. Not in this small place with two old women. But he calls on us when he is back from his travels. Doesn't he, Katerina? He is a good boy, isn't he?"

"*Ja, ja, ja!*"

"He travels a lot?" Grace asked. She took the cup of coffee offered her, holding it carefully, afraid the cup would rattle against the saucer.

"A great deal. To all sorts of places, Jutland, Norway, Finland, sometimes to Baltic ports. He is captain of a ship. Axel has done well, hasn't he, Katerina?"

"He's married?" Grace asked.

Anna shook her head, laughing. The joke

seemed to be a good one, "*Nej, nej, nej.* How would he have been interested in Froken Bedford if he had had a wife?"

The coffee was too strong and bitter. Grace gulped it, wishing for Polsen to hear this conversation.

"He liked Willa?"

"I think a little. But then he objected to the colour she had made her hair. It was a very strong colour. Axel has serious views, and thought it unsuitable. I believe they parted not the best of friends."

"What a shame," said Grace. "Is your nephew good-looking?"

The bait was taken with ridiculous ease.

"You must see a picture of him. Look! Look at this!"

"What are you getting, Anna?" Katerina asked inquisitively.

"The picture of Axel on his twenty-first birthday. Mind you, that was twelve years ago. He is much more serious now. He smiles less."

He was not smiling too much in this photograph either. He had a long chin, a long straight nose, cool pale eyes.

He was not remotely like the mincing effeminate picture of Gustav IV.

"Yes, he is very good-looking," Grace said politely. "When will he be visiting you again?"

"We never know. It might be one month, two months, three months between visits. He comes and he goes, like a wild goose before the winter." Anna liked her poetic fancy and repeated it, adding with a gentle chuckle, "Not that Axel is a goose. He is much too clever."

Grace stood up. She seemed to have learned a great deal, but nothing that answered any questions. Except that Axel was not Gustav.

What had Willa written in her diary about him?

Axel staring at me with that awful dire seriousness. Too boring for words.

"Come and see us again, Miss Asherton," Anna said, tilting her little white-parrot head, and Katerina echoed, "So kind."

The door closed and the old ladies vanished, an old-fashioned cosy daguerreotype put back in a drawer.

But why hadn't Polsen told her about Axel?

Because he never saw what was under his nose, he admitted shamefacedly. He knew the old ladies had a nephew, but he had always been referred to by Fru Lindstrom and others as Captain Morgensson, never as Axel.

How had Grace got into that parlour with those two pussy cats? It was something he had never done. He didn't believe Willa had either. Nor did he believe Willa could have seen the nephew more than a couple of times. Hadn't she written that he was too boring for words? He couldn't be Gustav. Could he?

Grace said her head was full of cotton wool. She was glad she was going to have a long drive with the Sinclairs in the fresh air to-morrow.

Polsen looked hurt. What had they been doing all day that day? But he admitted that it was a good idea for Grace to be looked after by the Sinclairs, because on Sundays he always took his son out. He never let anything upset this arrangement.

"You mustn't feel you have to be responsible for me," Grace said. Her voice sounded spikier than she had meant it to be. Of course Polsen's son must come before such a new acquaintance as herself, and her improbable problems.

This conversation had taken place at the top of the stairs outside her door, and she was tired and cold. Her elation about Axel had very quickly passed. It was a clue that had led to nothing.

"Me! It seems I'm too stupid to be responsible even for myself," Polsen said, still brooding over his obtuseness about the Misses Morgensson's nephew. "Don't rely on me to recognise Gustav until he is right under my nose."

All the same, he didn't quite look at her, and she could see that secret awareness in his eyes. She decided that she had never had the least idea what he was thinking.

6

"SO you intend staying on," Peter Sinclair said. With a touch of irritability, Grace thought. But the atmosphere in the car had not yet thawed out. It was almost as chilly as the morning. What seemed like a half gale was blowing across the lake, rocking the little neat boats at their moorings, and sending leaves spinning along the pavement.

Kate had a scarf tied round her head, concealing her hair and making her face look sharp and diminished. Peter, on the other hand, wore such a wide-shouldered sweater that he seemed twice his size. His thick fair hair was blown about. He looked healthy and attractive except for the bad humour he couldn't quite dismiss, even when Grace had got into the car.

The children wore red tam-o'-shanters which were too gay for their pale solemn faces. Georgy was in a talkative mood, happy to be having the day out, but Alexander sat quite silent in his corner. He was frightened of elks, Georgy said. Wasn't that silly, especially when it wasn't likely they would see any. He had to get over that sort of nonsense, his father said over his shoulder, and then asked Grace the question about staying on in Stockholm.

Before she could answer, however, her attention was diverted by a tall man and a small boy who had just crossed the road.

"Look, Peter! That's Polsen!"

She looked back, ready to wave, but Polsen was totally engrossed in what the small boy was saying. His absorbed face seemed to be not the one she knew at all. Although how could she possibly be so sure of that in a split-second glimpse?

"Is that his boy?" Peter asked.

"I expect so."

"You didn't say that he had a wife and child."

"He doesn't live with them. He takes his son out on Sundays."

"Oh, that sort of thing," said Kate.

"The divorce rate in Sweden is the highest in the world," said Peter. "You know that, darling."

"Yes, but there's no need to discuss it now. Little pitchers."

"That's us," Georgy said to Grace. "What's a divorce rate?"

"Never mind," said Kate sharply. "Grace, you didn't answer Peter's question. Do you mean to stay on?"

"Until I hear from Willa, yes."

"But if she doesn't know you're here, love," Peter said mildly. "She may be in Copenhagen, Paris, Rome, Rio de Janeiro. Who knows?"

"She'll have to come back for her things and to settle about the flat. Besides I'm beginning to enjoy my holiday." Which was true, in an odd way, and in spite of the glimpse she had just caught of Polsen as a besotted parent. He ought to go back to his wife, the old fool.

"Fancy staying here from preference," Kate grumbled.

The sky was clear except for a low bank of luminous grey clouds on the horizon. Snow clouds, Peter said. They might roll up later in the day. At this time of the year, everyone talked about snow and prepared for it, but one never knew when it would begin. The birch trees flared like torches among the sombre green spruce and pines. In less than half an hour after leaving the city they were

96

driving through the forest, broken here and there by clearings where the doll-sized cottages, so loved by the city-bound Swedes, had been built. Occasionally the forest opened out to give glimpses of lake water, or it thinned away altogether and there were flat sodden fields with great outcrops of rock, as if the bones of this harsh country were showing.

"This is the road to Uppsala," Peter said. "You must go there one day. It has a university and a fine cathedral. We branch off presently, and go down towards the lake."

"It's near here that Ebba and Jacob live," Kate said. "Of course, they have a mansion, not a poky cottage."

"A Gothic pile," Peter said. "I hope they'll invite you to it, Grace. And it's their official residence, not a summer cottage. You weren't thinking we could rent one like that, Kate? My wife's a dreamer, Grace. She's not with you half the time. She's back in Surbiton. Aren't you, love?"

"There!" exclaimed Georgy. "Did you see it, Grace? That sign said 'Beware of elks!' Didn't it, Daddy?"

"Did it? I missed it."

"But it did. You said so other times. Did you know that elks have horns, Grace? That's why Alexander is scared of them. They horn you and throw you in the air and then stamp on you."

"Georgy! Stop it!" Kate said.

Alexander cringed in his corner, his eyes wide as he stared into the shadowy forest.

"They could have done it to Willa," Georgy muttered.

"Watch it!" said her father. "Or you'll find yourself spending the day in the bedroom, my girl."

"If she *is* lost in the forest," Georgy finished in a determined whisper.

THE COTTAGE was in a wide clearing, the forest sufficiently hidden behind a screen of young birches and wild roses and brambles to restore Alexander's confidence. He erupted out of the car and began running in wide circles, Georgy following, both of them screaming with laughter.

"Well, thank goodness for that," Peter said. "I don't know what's got into Alexander about elks."

"It was that last one you shot," Kate answered. "He saw blood on it. After all, he is only four."

"Going on five. Can't have him go green at

the sight of a bit of blood. Well, this is our mansion, Grace. It won't take you long to look over it."

Yet it was attractive for all its small size. Two rooms, one a bedroom with four bunks, the other a kitchen-dining-living room, comfortable with its scrubbed floor and plain furniture.

"When Willa stayed, she had one of the bunks with the girls and Alexander and I slept on the couch in here," Peter said.

The silence was profound. No rain drumming on the roof, no dark trees crowding the house.

"Did she stay often?" Grace asked.

"Only once," said Kate. "We intended to have her again, but there never was another opportunity. Either she had other plans, or Peter came down with Bill—with men friends to go elk shooting."

Bill? That was a new name. Kate seemed to regret using it. It had been a slip of the tongue.

Grace was afraid that her questions were going to make her unpopular.

"Bill? Who is he? One of Willa's boy friends?"

"Goodness gracious, she wasn't *that* attractive!" Kate burst out waspishly. "When she dyed her hair that canary colour I thought she was decidedly common. It was rather a relief, wasn't it, Peter, when she decided to go?"

"Well, I told her if she stayed she'd have to tone down a bit," Peter admitted.

"So this Bill couldn't have had anything to do with her going?" Grace persisted stubbornly.

"Hardly," Peter's voice was curt. He was looking out of the window across the clearing into the dusky forest. "Since he's dead."

"Dead!" Grace said uncertainly, looking from Kate to Peter, wondering why neither of them seemed to want to say anything more.

"You'd better tell her," Kate said at last. "Otherwise Georgy will. In her own inimitable fashion. That child has the weirdest imagination."

"There was an accident when Bill was out looking for elk." Peter said in a suddenly hard-clipped voice. "Bill Jordan was one of my colleagues. Unmarried, fortunately, so we didn't have the ordeal of breaking the news to a wife."

"But how?" Grace asked.

"The usual sort of damned stupid shooting accident. He tripped in the undergrowth and

100

his gun went off. Got him in the stomach. He'd gone out alone. God knows how long he'd lain there before I found him. He couldn't tell me because he was dead by then."

"How perfectly awful!" Involuntarily the thought came to Grace that this must have been one of the scandals that the Embassy deplored.

"It was ghastly," said Kate. "I tried to keep it from the children, but of course they knew something had happened. Georgy thought an elk had attacked him, and that's why Alexander has had this obsession ever since."

Peter flung round, saying in a loud angry voice, "He's got to get over it. That's why I don't want any more talk of this. It was a tragedy, and I blame myself for not having gone with Bill that morning. I didn't realise he was such a novice. But what was I doing? I was sleeping off a hangover. We'd cracked a bottle of vodka the night before and Bill had a better head than me. Or perhaps he hadn't. Perhaps that's what made him stumble. But it's over. He can't be brought back. So no more talk, girls. Understand?"

Kate nodded, her eyes getting their haunted look.

"He always comes into my mind when we arrive here. But I make myself forget. Ugh, it's cold! Let's light the fire. Peter, bring in some logs while Grace and I get the food. It's really too late in the year to come down here. I wouldn't be surprised if it snowed before the day's out."

The fire in the pleasantly austere room was cheerful. The children sat on the hearthrug, Grace and Kate on the couch. Peter sprawled in the rocking chair, plucking at the strings of a guitar. When it was summer, he said, they spent most of the day down by the lake. In the warm evenings they sat on the doorstep and he played the guitar and anyone who could sang and the light never faded completely, even at midnight.

After lunch the children wanted to go down to the lake. Kate said they could go alone, then changed her mind and said she would go with them. You never knew, Alexander might do something crazy like falling in. Grace and Peter could stay and snooze by the fire if they were too lazy for a walk.

Peter said he certainly was too lazy. Grace would have liked the walk, but she decided to take the opportunity to tell Peter about the mysterious visitor to Willa's flat yesterday.

She preferred the children, with their so quickly strained eyes, Kate, too, for that matter, not to hear.

Peter looked at her silently while she told him. He didn't laugh sceptically. He frowned a little, his sandy brows drawn together, and asked Kate what she thought the intruder—if he existed outside her imagination—was looking for?

The diary? Grace regarded that as being as private as the secret signature on Willa's letter. If Peter knew about it he would want to read it. Intuition had made her happy enough to let Polsen read it. But Peter was at once too flippant and too much the heavy boss to allow him to see that curious outpouring. Not at this stage, anyway.

"I don't know. Letters, perhaps. Something that would incriminate him. Winifred Wright talked about a married man. It's all a bit sordid, isn't it?"

"Mucky," said Peter. He reflected, his arms folded behind his head. He was only attractive when he was animated and laughing. "Have you had a good look round in the flat yourself?"

"Yes, I have."

"Found anything?"

"Nothing of significance. And yet too much. All those perfectly good clothes. Make-up things, that scent that was spilled. Suitcases. Willa must have been living beyond her income."

"And now she's having another shopping spree, I expect. She must have found herself a millionaire."

"If she has," said Grace, after a pause, "that's surely a story the newspapers will want to use."

"Sure. Let them ferret it out."

"In the meantime, I'm having the lock of the door changed. I don't care to have someone with a spare key wandering about."

"You're really thinking up a mystery, aren't you, love?"

Grace frowned, curling up on the hearthrug, wrapping her arms round herself in a chilly way, in spite of the heat of the fire.

"I don't need to think it up. It's been one from the moment I arrived."

"Daddy! Daddy!" shouted Georgy. "Look what we found!"

The children had burst in, followed by Kate. Georgy was thrusting a muddy object into her father's hands. He took it gingerly, looking up enquiringly at his wife.

"It's only a pair of sun glasses," she said. She was looking pinched and pale in spite of her walk. "Georgy spotted them in the mud at the edge of the lake."

"But they're Willa's, Daddy!" Georgy declared. "She always wore them."

Peter scraped some mud off the tortoise-shell frames. He stared at the glasses thoughtfully, no expression on his face.

"I expect there are plenty of this kind about. They aren't necessarily Willa's. If she had lost them she'd have said so."

"Perhaps she did say so," Kate murmured, in a tight voice.

Peter looked at her.

"Darling, if you're suggesting—"

Kate signalled violently for him to be quiet. She turned to the children and said in an unnaturally bright voice, "Willa must have been here some time when we weren't. That's why we didn't know about her losing her glasses. That is, if they are hers. We aren't sure of that."

"But they are, Mummy," Georgy insisted. "Look, they're made like a butterfly. Willa used to show us. Didn't she, Alexander?"

"So is she truly lost in the forest?" Alexander asked, his too large eyes comical in his small freckled face.

"Alexander, will you stop that nonsense!" Peter exclaimed thunderously. "Kate, can't you get him out of this whining."

"I weren't whining," Alexander protested, his knuckles dug in his eyes. Kate silently folded him in her arms, while Peter muttered, more quietly, something about the boy being outrageously spoilt.

Grace put her hand out for the mud-encrusted glasses. "I'll take those. I'll keep them for Willa."

Did Peter hesitate? Almost at once he said, "If you want them. They only look fit to chuck away—lying in that stinking mud."

All the way home Kate didn't say a word. Her profile was sharp, tense, unforgiving. She was obviously quite convinced that Peter had taken Willa to the cottage, unknown to her, on one of the weekends when she had imagined he was with his men friends, elk hunting. That was a quarrel husband and wife would have to sort out. More significantly to Grace, it was now clear that Peter knew more about Willa than he was prepared to say. Well, she had no intention of prying into his indiscretions, unless they had any bearing on Willa's whereabouts. The dark glasses could well have been lost some time ago. It would have been easy enough to replace them. All this must have happened in the summer, long before the present mystery.

Now it was nearly winter, the wind had a knife edge and as the twilight advanced the flaring light of the birches went out, leaving the forest quite dark. Although the ballooning grey clouds had rolled up and were now touched with an icy silver light, it did not seem as if any snow was going to fall that evening.

7

GRACE wouldn't go up to see Polsen when she arrived home. He had never invited her into his rooms. Not that there had been much time for him to do so, she told herself fairly. She had only known him two days.

But he had told her that Sundays were sacrosanct to Magnus, and she had no intention of encroaching on them. Not even, she said to herself, if it had been Willa's body they had found by the lake.

"It was only her glasses, Polsen. But they were covered with mud, and creepy! Really creepy. When did you last see her wearing those butterfly glasses?"

Grace couldn't stop shivering as she walked about Willa's flat talking aloud. She had drawn all the curtains to shut out a high glittering moon moving behind the great snowclouds, and had switched on all the lights. The bedroom still smelled of the Balenciaga perfume. It was, however, completely orderly, and exactly as she had left it that morning. The intruder had not been back.

Willa, of course, as Peter had said, must have bought another pair of glasses.

Exactly the same? Well, why not. If a shop had one pair, it very likely had several. Tomorrow she must go shopping for dark glasses with tortoiseshell rims shaped like a butterfly. Where would Willa be most likely to shop? At the nearest chemist's, or at a big department store like N.K.? Fru Lindstrom might know. She might even remember Willa complaining about losing her glasses.

(But wouldn't she have gone back to look for them? They would surely have been easy enough to find by the lake where she had been swimming.)

And if there were none of that particular make available in the shops, if Grace was told they had never been stocked, that they must have been bought in England, then it would be clear that Willa had lost them very recently, as recently as her departure on her presumed honeymoon . . .

Grace went into the bathroom and held the glasses under a running tap, scouring them fiercely with a hard-bristled brush to remove every last vestige of mud. When dried, she put them on reflectively and was startled by the way her face had changed, grown enigmatic, almost invisible. Was that the answer to Willa's sudden idiosyncrasy about wearing dark glasses, that she wanted to be invisible. Surely not extrovert Willa!

The unfamiliar face looked back at her from the bathroom mirror in a haze of muted green. Let's get into Willa's personality further, she suddenly decided, and stripping off her slacks and sweater, she riffled through the clothes in the wardrobe. The gold dress? No, not that, but the extravagantly wide-legged jersey silk trouser suit was a suitable lounging garment for an evening at home.

The canary hair could not be simulated. Grace compromised by brushing her own dark spiky locks back from her face, and pinning them in a skinny topknot. She applied pale lipstick generously. The silk jersey felt luxurious against her skin. She was lost in the flowing trousers, an undersized femme fatale, with the dark glasses swallowing up her face.

So this was being Willa, a creature in disguise, putting on an act of being someone far more interesting and irresistible than a secretary, until finally she was caught permanently in her act.

But it was fun, Grace realised reluctantly. She almost felt gay and irresponsible herself, which was a strange and heady emotion. Perhaps she ought to stop being so much herself, to escape outside her own skin occasionally.

"Come in, Axel, Sven, Jacob, Gustav—whoever you all are," she said loudly, and the door opened and Polsen walked in.

She had to take off her glasses to see him properly. As she did so he said grimly, "That's better. Now get out of the rest of that gear. Fast."

"But, Polsen! I was only—"

"Only living in that damned fantasy Willa lived in! It doesn't suit you. Willa, perhaps. What was she without a fantasy? But not you, for God's sake! Besides, it's dangerous as well."

Dangerous? From a personality point of view, perhaps. Grace was thinking another thing, in mild surprise. Polsen hadn't liked Willa. And he definitely wasn't expecting her to come back. The shock in his face had given him away.

"I didn't invite you in," Grace said sulkily from the bedroom.

"You did. I distinctly heard your voice saying come in."

"I didn't hear you knock, and you weren't invited in. Anyway, this is Sunday and you're supposed to be with your son."

His voice was calmer. "It is nine o'clock, if you will look at the time, and Magnus has been in bed one hour exactly. Now! I call that an improvement."

This was because Grace had appeared in her red woollen dressing gown, and with the pins taken out of her hair.

"I'm sorry I spoke so rudely. I just didn't care to see you dressed in that vulgar way."

"Did you think Willa vulgar?" Grace asked.

"Of course. It suited her. It doesn't suit you. And I only came to ask if you had noticed the bolt I had put on your door. Fru Lindstrom allowed me to use her key, and Magnus and I did this for you. It works from the inside, so you will feel quite safe until the lock is changed." His voice altered. "What's that you've got?"

"Willa's glasses," Grace said swinging them in her hand. She knew he had recog-

112

nised them. She had heard the sharp aware note in his voice.

"You didn't find them here!"

"Why do you say that? Because you knew Willa only has one pair and she's never without them? But perhaps she bought another pair after she lost these. She must have done, because the children found them today by the lake, covered in mud, and Peter Sinclair said they must have been there all summer."

He stared at the glasses, frowning deeply. Once again Grace found his enigmatic expression infuriating. Why couldn't he tell her what he was thinking?

"Well? Do you think that, too?" she said impatiently.

"How am I to know? My eyesight isn't perfect. I could have sworn they were the glasses Willa was wearing the last time I saw her. That wasn't the beginning of the summer."

"Kate Sinclair thought her husband and Willa had been down to the cottage alone."

"Did she say so?"

"She didn't have to *say* so. I could read her face. She's unhappy and not just because she wants to go back to England. If she was jealous of Willa, she no longer has any need to be. But she still goes on brooding and the children are upset and edgy, and Peter goes off for weekends shooting alone. Or presumably alone."

Polsen nodded slowly.

"I see. Then if Willa lost these glasses early in the summer, she must have been able to buy another pair exactly the same."

Grace didn't bother to say that his reasoning was elementary.

"I thought I'd try a few shops tomorrow."

"A good idea. You ought to be able to find out whether that kind is sold here. They aren't so ordinary. So tell me, what else happened today? Was it a pleasant day?"

Grace was thinking overwhelmingly of the chilly lakeside, the surrounding forest. Like Alexander she was getting an obsession about the forest.

"Polsen, do you remember a young man from the British Embassy being accidentally killed when he was elk shooting? Called Bill Jordan."

"I remember, of course. It was only a few weeks ago. There were headlines about it. British diplomat in tragic accident. That sort of thing."

"But you're saying it as if you don't believe a word! It really was true. Peter told me about finding the body. It must have been horrible."

"Oh, I'm not saying the poor fellow wasn't dead. I only don't believe the official report. Nor did many other people."

"Suicide?" Grace had a sense of shock, unreasonably severe.

"That was more likely than that a man who could handle a gun should accidentally shoot himself in the stomach."

"I see. It had to be hushed up. No scandal in the Embassy. Was there any talk of anything in Bill Jordan's private life that would make him do such a thing?"

"That could be hushed up, too. How would I know, except that Willa seemed to think it an unnecessary tragedy. She said Bill Jordan was nice, everyone liked him, he hadn't stolen the petty cash. Why? That was what she said, too."

"*I can't bear those cemeteries full of tall trees and short gravestones.*" Willa had written. "*They are too melancholy. They make the trees so important and us so unimportant . . .*"

Us . . .

Grace sprang up.

"Have a drink, Polsen. I need one. Whisky? And what did you do today? You and Magnus?"

"Oh, many things." Instantly he was another person, his expression soft and reminiscent. (You look daft when you go all sentimental like that, Grace wanted to say scathingly.) "Magnus, for one thing, has an extremely large appetite. After lunch we went to see the Haga Pavilion. Now that's a place for you to see, Grace. It was built by Gustav III in the French manner. It's small and elegant. There's a mirror room and a library, and a lot of steep stairs up to very small attics where it is said that Gustav kept his queen. She would, of course, get a fine view over the lake."

"What did you say?" Grace asked, pausing with the whisky bottle in her hand.

"She would get a fine view."

"No—about the attics. *The queen in the attic*. That's in Willa's diary."

"So it is. But I assure you, those attics are quite empty."

"Another attic. Somewhere else. Someone shut up. Polsen, am I going mad?"

116

He came towards her and ruffled her hair. His big hand was heavy on her head. Reassuring.

"You, with this cool sensible head? Of course you're not going mad. But don't get too much caught in Willa's fantasy. Look at it dispassionately."

"It's getting beyond being dispassionate. It's making me feel creepy. And it's too quiet in this room when I'm alone. I have to talk aloud."

"Then don't stay in it too much. Tomorrow morning, while I take my class at the university, you shall go shopping for dark glasses. In the afternoon I can spare some time to take you over to the old town."

"To look for the door with the dragon?" Grace asked.

"Is that the next item on our list?"

Grace began to laugh shakily. "You make it seem like a game. You're enjoying playing it."

He gave her an indulgent smile. She guessed that that was the way he smiled at his son. Well, it was better than indifference. But Willa, with her sexy vulgarity, would not have been looked at as if she were a child.

NO BUTTERFLY GLASSES. The blank stares met Grace everywhere. *Nej*, such glasses had not been bought in this shop. They were not Swedish, *froken*. Imported, perhaps, but where they could be bought, no one knew.

Grace rang Fru Lindstrom's doorbell, deliberately wearing the glasses. That lady gave a great start, her eyes popping.

"Goodness gracious, Froken Asherton, I thought at first that you were Froken Bedford. You have the same glasses."

Grace took the glasses off, her experiment too successful. Why did everyone seem so startled at the thought of Willa appearing? She hated these glasses. They made the world look a mouldy sinister green.

"My cousin always wore them, didn't she? Did you ever see her without them?"

"For going to work, yes. But usually in the evenings or at weekends she had them on. She wore them like—you know—" she patted her cheeks "—make-up."

"Was there a time in the summer when she didn't wear them?"

"*Nej.* I didn't notice. Why do you ask?"

"I thought she might have lost them and had to get some more."

"I never heard of her losing them."

"Then was she wearing them the day she left here?"

Fru Lindstrom considered. "I think not," she said at last. "She had her coat with the fur collar and a fur hat to match. She looked very nice, very smart. No, I remember that she wasn't wearing her glasses because I saw how her eyes shone. I thought what a pity it was to always hide them behind dark glass. Like a blind person. She wasn't blind, your cousin."

"Was someone waiting for her that day?" Grace asked, wondering why she hadn't asked that question before. Gustav? Perhaps Fru Lindstrom had actually set eyes on him.

But she hadn't. She shook her head. "She went in a taxi. She must have telephoned for it. She waved to me and was gone. I was too far off to hear what address she gave the driver."

Fru Lindstrom wasn't in the least ashamed of admitting her curiosity. But in a moment her expression changed to suspicion.

"What are all these questions about? Was Froken Bedford wearing her glasses and so on? You have her glasses in your hand."

"I only wanted to know if she had two pairs," Grace said. "I found these," she added offhandedly, and knew her explanation

119

must sound lame. "Thank you, Fru Lindstrom. I'm sorry to have troubled you."

"But it isn't trouble. I enjoy a conversation. You are always welcome. This is a quiet house. Herre Polsen is always busy and the old ladies are too hard of hearing to make conversing a pleasure."

"Then I expect you enjoy it when their nephew comes home."

"Captain Morgensson? *Ja*. He is a charming man. He has a wife in every port, I expect. And stays free. You must meet him. But take him with a grain of salt, eh? That's what Froken Bedford did."

Did she? Or did she call him Gustav and run off with him because he had made her pregnant and she would not have an abortion? The diary said that he was too boring for words. But that might have been a deliberately misleading statement.

THE MIDDAY SKY was clear and cold, the sunlight like yellow glass across the arm of the lake. The little boats tilted in the wind. Grace watered the plants in Willa's window boxes, wondering if Willa had really meant to leave them to die. Then she sat at the little writing desk (where Willa had written her

120

curious hysterical diary?) and wrote postcards to a few friends. *Having a fascinating holiday. Stockholm interesting, the Swedes also, in varying degrees.* This completely ordinary task soothed her jangled nerves, and almost made her believe that she was having a normal holiday.

She wrote at greater length to her father. He lived (with an ailing heart that made him a semi-invalid) in a cottage in Wiltshire, cultivating dahlias, going for short unexhausting walks with his elderly spaniel and two Siamese cats, and keeping his daily woman, who had designs on him, at bay. He enjoyed Grace's visits, and wanted to hear everything of her life that she was prepared to tell him. His marriage hadn't been particularly happy, and he was glad that his daughter didn't take after her mother or her aunt. That relationship had been too much for him. Perhaps it was for that reason that he had never liked Willa. She was too trendy, too phoney. Grace might make a mess, occasionally, of her emotional life (what sensitive person didn't?), but she could be depended on to behave with good sense. Willa would follow disastrous paths, like that abortion tragedy, and drag other people with her.

Grace had no right to fly off to Sweden because she imagined Willa had some serious problem.

But he understood she had to go, being the person of integrity that she was. He and his spaniel and the cats would be there whenever she liked to come down.

The thought of that peaceful environment was as soothing to Grace as writing the innocuous postcards had been. It was out of the question that she could tell that gentle delicate man melodramatic things like queens shut in attics, or bloody elk hunts or the presumed suicide of a minor embassy official—or of the discovery of Willa's glasses half-buried in mud on the lakeshore. He would ask her if she were out of her mind. But it would worry him. So she wrote, "I promise that as soon as Willa comes back with this husband whom I can't wait to meet I'll be back in England and down for a few days. I must start a new book. I need some quiet country rambles. The Swedish countryside is too gloomy at this time of year, soggy and dark, and there's a perpetual threat of snow . . ."

There, she was herself again, Grace Asherton, that intelligent promising novelist with

122

her serious face, wispy dark hair, slightly forlorn mouth. Unsexy, sensible, dedicated, emotions in control . . . And forgetting the spurious excitement of Willa's trouser suit, and scent, and dyed hair and butterfly-shaped glasses that turned the world as mysterious as her own face.

By the time she had finished her letters it was time to get lunch, a cold snack of lettuce and tomatoes and a hard-boiled egg and coffee. Then the man to put the new lock on the door had arrived. He was a solemn young fellow who seemed to think the work unnecessary. There was a perfectly good lock already. When Grace explained about the duplicate key he nodded understandingly and said, *ja, ja,* there was a great deal of crime in the city. He saw the evidence of it in his job.

"I suppose you know the city very well?" Grace said.

He agreed that he did, and suggested that if she wanted directions as to any street or house she had only to ask him.

"The house in the old town with the carved dragon on the door," she said glibly, testing him. "Who does that belong to? Someone important?"

"Near the Square?"

"Yes, that's it," Grace said, making a guess.

"That's Doctor Backe."

The Backes in their Strindberg house. Sven and Ulrika. So Sven was a doctor!

The man began talking about the statue of St. George killing the dragon on the foreshore. It was very old. Most foreigners went to look at that. It was a particularly fine and fearsome dragon, much more spectacular than only a door knocker.

Grace nodded absently, making her plan about visiting Doctor Backe. Forewarned was forearmed. Polsen would admire her acumen. He would also have to co-operate. If he refused, she supposed she would have to go alone. She was sure there was nothing to be frightened about. But she preferred to have his company.

"So you are having my baby and I ask you to kill it!" She had never heard him speak with such outrage. "What sort of a man do you take me for?"

Impulsively she threw her arms round him, liking him for his indignation, even though it was for a hypothetical reason.

"Polsen, don't take it so seriously. We're only pretending. It's only a ploy."

"But not one I will associate myself with. I'm sorry, Grace. I live here. I'm known."

"Do you know this Doctor Backe?"

"No, but—"

"Then why should he know you?"

"He may not, but he may, and it isn't only that. I would never ask my girl to lose my baby."

"I'm not your girl," Grace pointed out. "And anyway this doctor wouldn't talk. He wouldn't dare to. It's only that I want to see his reaction when I ask for an abortion. To see if that's why Willa went to him."

"I know, but you have to realise that she might have been under some pressure."

Polsen began to pace up and down the room, his head bent, glowering.

"No, I can't do it, Grace. Not even for you. But I'll sit in the square and wait for you. If you don't come out of the house in a reasonable time, I'll ring the bell and ask for you."

"As who?"

"As my wife, of course."

"You'll do that, Polsen?"

"Reluctantly."

"Thank you. That'll be just fine. It was silly of me to be scared to do this alone."

125

"As if I could play a part like that convincingly," he grumbled, "when I would have liked to be the father of ten children."

He added, "What about the spectacles?"

"No luck. They're English. or French. Or maybe American."

"So Willa had two pairs."

"I expect so."

She must have had, or otherwise she might just possibly be at the bottom of that octopus arm of Lake Malaren. But that was an inadmissible fancy, belonging to the nightmare category.

A girl who didn't look more than sixteen, although she must have been more because she wore a nurse's uniform, opened the door of the house in the narrow dark street. Grace had enjoyed rapping the door knocker, the small golden dragon with a splendid curly tail. She had done so firmly, telling herself that she wasn't in the least nervous.

She had given a backward glance at Polsen, sitting in the distance on a bench in the cobbled square, his coat collar hunched round his ears. It was reassuring to see him there. She had finally agreed that it was wiser to play this act in this absurd Willa-type farce alone.

She asked if she could see Doctor Backe. She hadn't an appointment. She spoke in a low urgent voice, pretending anxiety, and was thankful when the girl understood her and answered in good English.

The doctor was out on a call, but if Grace cared to come in and wait she was welcome. The girl led the way, her thin figure slightly stooped, her hair twisted in a lank pony tail. She was unattractive and aware of it, poor kid, for she was quite without poise. She sat at a desk in the corner of the room, her head bent over some work.

"I was recommended to come here by my cousin," Grace said, when the silence had become too oppressive.

The girl looked up. "Yes?"

"My cousin, Willa Bedford. She worked at the British Embassy."

The sudden movement of the girl's hand to her mouth, her startled eyes.

"Yes?" she said again.

"You remember her? When was she here?"

"I don't remember exactly. A few weeks ago. But she wasn't sick. At least, the doctor didn't prescribe for her." The girl was mumbling, her head down. "Hasn't she told you that herself?"

"I haven't seen her. She had gone off on her wedding trip, or whatever it is, before I arrived in Stockholm. I'm awfully anxious to find out where she's gone."

"Is that why you've come to the doctor?" the girl asked suspiciously. "Why do you think Sven knows anything about your cousin?"

But he must know something, for this girl was suddenly too nervous. In her nervousness, she had, surely unintentionally, called the doctor by his christian name.

"I only intend to ask him," Grace said, and got no farther, for there were voices in the passage, quite audible through the closed door. A man's and a woman's, the woman's with its confident throaty tone tantalisingly familiar.

Frustratingly they were speaking in Swedish. Grace heard the name Ulrika, and a little later that of Jacob and instantly knew who the woman with the purring voice was. The Baroness von Sturpe.

The nurse had got up and slid to the door. Opening it a crack, she said something rapidly. There was a moment's silence, then the man's voice said with professional briskness, "*Tak*, Ebba. *Farval.*"

128

"*Farval*, Sven."

The street door slammed. Grace wondered if Polsen was watching the tall slender figure of the Baroness walking away. Not that there was any particular significance in Doctor Sven Backe and Ebba von Sturpe being friends.

Or was there? For the door of the small dark waiting room was thrown open and the tall man who stood revealed was giving Grace a highly critical and penetrating stare.

"Miss Asherton?" he said in excellent English. "You wish to consult me?"

"Not about my own health," Grace had made an instant change of plan. "About my cousin's, Miss Bedford's. I'm worried about her. I know she came to see you and I thought you might be able to relieve my mind about her."

The man had a taut dark face, dark intense eyes, thinning dark hair. He was a change from all the blonde Swedes, at least.

"Relieve your mind?" he didn't understand the expression, or pretended not to. "Come this way, Miss Asherton."

The thin nurse pressed herself against the wall, like a cut-out paper doll. Grace followed the doctor past her up a short flight of stairs and into a clean, efficient, well-lighted surgery. A wide desk, a couple of leather-covered chairs, some photographs on the mantelpiece, a hard narrow bed covered with a white sheet along the wall.

Grace was deeply thankful that she had given up the abortion plan. She might have had to climb on to that bed. She had an instant and unreasonable aversion to this dark gloomily handsome man touching her, professionally or otherwise.

"Sit down," Doctor Backe said. His voice was curt. If he had a bedside manner he was not using it for her. "Now what is it you want to ask me?"

"I think Willa must be having some sort of mental illness," Grace said. "She would never behave like this otherwise. I mean, going off secretly to be married and not telling anyone who she was marrying. It simply isn't like her, is it?"

Doctor Backe gave a faint smile. "How do you think I can answer that question?"

"You knew her, didn't you?"

"What makes you think that, Miss Asherton?"

"Because she wrote about you," Grace said

smoothly. "In letters. Sven and Ulrika, she said. Is Ulrika your wife?"

"My sister," he said in a clipped voice. "I suppose your cousin mentioned visiting us. It was one weekend in the summer. We had a house party. I'm afraid I don't remember her awfully well, all the same."

A lie, Grace thought. Men always remembered Willa.

"Was Gustav there, too?" she asked casually.

"Gustav?"

"This man Willa is supposed to have married. Why does nobody know him? Or does everybody know him?"

A nerve twitched in the man's cheek. He stood up abruptly.

"I can't help you, Miss Asherton. I'm flattered that your cousin should mention me in a letter, but we weren't close friends, and she didn't confide in me about her personal life. If you must know why she came here to consult me, it was about her pregnancy . . . I am not accustomed to giving details about my patients, but as you are a relation and seem unnecessarily anxious I can tell you that much. She is a healthy girl and should have a healthy child."

"We found her sunglasses by the lake," Grace said, with apparent irrelevancy. "Near the Sinclairs' house. Would that be near your house, too?"

The dark moody eyes looked down at her. "We have a house at Sigtuna. Quite twenty miles away." He made no comment about the glasses. Grace was almost certain that he already knew about that discovery. "I'm sorry I can't help you any more, Miss Asherton. And I shall have to ask you to excuse me. I have an urgent call to make." His expression was severe. "These are not my surgery hours. My nurse should have told you so."

Grace had left her coat and gloves in the small reception room. She went back to get them, and the thin nurse gave a convulsive start as she entered. She was sitting on the edge of her chair looking as if she would like to have been listening at the keyhole.

"It's all right," Grace said reassuringly. The girl with those popping eyes was like a startled hare. "My cousin was ill. At least not ill but pregnant. She really did want to see a doctor."

"Oh! Oh, yes!" The girl stared, fascinated, as Grace buttoned her coat and tied a scarf round her head. Poor Polsen sitting outdoors would be frozen. There was little enough to tell him except that Sven Backe was darkly handsome, but bore no resemblance to Gustav IV except, perhaps, in character. And that he was strangely anxious to disclaim friendship with Willa.

There was a rustle behind her and the nurse was suddenly saying rapidly, in a whisper, "It was more than that. I shouldn't tell you. But it's so much on my mind. Your cousin was upset about the young man who died in the forest. She sat in this room and cried."

"But why come here?" Grace found herself also speaking in a whisper.

"Because Doctor Backe was called to the body. Your cousin wanted to know—she begged him to tell her—if Herre Jordan had been murdered."

"Murdered!"

The girl nodded rapidly.

"Yes, yes. But your cousin was mistaken, of course. It was an accident. Doctor Backe said so. I heard their conversation."

"And she didn't mention her baby to the doctor that day?" Grace said slowly.

"*Nej*. She was not thinking of babies just then. I can tell you that."

Grace turned to go. She turned back. "Why have you told me this?"

"Because your cousin seemed frightened, Miss Asherton. Awfully frightened."

"Not like someone going to be married?"

"Oh, no. Not at all like that. And now you see she's gone, and the doctor hasn't told you the truth and I simply don't know why."

"It's nothing for you to worry about." Grace heard footsteps in the room over their heads and spoke in a clear voice, at the door. "Thank you for your directions. It's awfully kind of you. I always get lost in a strange city."

Accident? Suicide? Murder?

It wasn't the mystery of Bill Jordan's death but the mystery of Willa's disappearance they had to solve.

Grace hurried across the cobblestones, making sure she was out of sight of the door with the carved dragon before breaking into a run to reach Polsen's side.

"It's Sven, Polsen! Doctor Backe is Sven. Ulrika is his sister. And Ebba was there. All those people seem to know each other."

"That's not surprising, Stockholm isn't such a large city." Polsen looked cold. His nose and cheeks were pink. He put one arm round Grace's shoulders, drawing her against him as if to protect her from the chilly wind.

"But *you* don't know them," Grace said. She looked up at his wind-bitten face. "Or do you?"

"I'm not a social fellow. I don't move in such circles. I don't move in circles at all. I have my work and my son." His eyes had their withdrawn look which forbade personal questions or pity. He was pretty thin-skinned, silly old Polsen, for all his detached manner.

"Before we freeze let's find a place to have some food. You can tell me everything then. And do me a favour, as you English say. Stop looking at me as if you don't trust me."

"Can I trust anybody?"

"Ah, now. Don't you think you are turning all this into a Gothic fairy tale?"

"Murder?"

His arm tightened round her sharply.

"I should have come with you after all. I'm sorry. Is this the murder of Willa's baby? Or an imaginary one?"

"Oh, it's nothing to do with abortion. That's simple compared with this. It refers to Bill Jordan."

Polsen made only an irrelevant remark.

"Your hand is like a small cold herring. Let's get indoors as quickly as possible."

THEY SAT in a dimly-lit cellar with oubliettes set high in thick stone walls. It was a warm and surprisingly cheerful place, in spite of its obviously grim past. Polsen ordered schnapps and onion soup.

"Now we'll talk in facts," he said. "Not in wild assumptions. Has someone just given you proof that Bill Jordan was murdered?"

"Not proof, of course. But Willa knew something about it. She was frightened, the nurse said."

"The nurse? I thought you went to see the doctor."

Grace bent her head over her bowl of soup. The steam warmed her face. The schnapps had already warmed her stomach. She was getting over her panic and beginning to think logically again.

"I believe that that girl is in love with Doctor Sven Backe and she's in a state of jitters because he was the doctor who gave medical evidence at the inquest. If there's a rumour going about that Bill Jordan's death wasn't an accident, then it's just possible Doctor Backe knows more than he's saying."

136

"So his loyal nurse who is in love with him spreads this nasty gossip?"

"No, not in that way." Grace looked at Polsen and said starkly, "She'd never have opened her mouth except that she's petrified about what's happened to Willa."

"So," Polsen murmured non-committally, "I won't be alarmed by your histrionics, Grace."

"So, suspecting the doctor as she does, if the girl wasn't in love with him she'd leave him, wouldn't she? She'd get another job with someone less mysterious."

"Has she any chance with the handsome doctor?"

"Oh, good heavens, none at all. She's so unremarkable, she's almost invisible. I mean, if he didn't particularly notice someone as flamboyant as Willa he isn't going to see this poor mouse."

"And Doctor Backe himself?"

"I got no further with him. He simply told me lies. Said Willa had come to him to confirm that she was expecting a baby. He said she would have a healthy child. Oh Polsen, I pray she does!"

Polsen ruffled his already untidy hair. He went off at another tangent.

"I have a piece of information for you. Captain Axel Morgensson's ship is due today or tomorrow."

Axel. The one with the cold eyes who stared . . .

"Is it really! Then what do we do?"

"We have to make his acquaintance."

"Do you think Willa might be on board his ship?"

Polsen properly ignored that fanciful remark, and said, "This is what we have to do, Grace. You have to give a party. I will share the expense."

She stared. "But I don't know anybody."

"A party for all Willa's friends. The people she knew at the Embassy, the Backes, Sven and Ulrika, Captain Axel Morgensson and his aunts, the von Sturpes—"

"The Baron, too!"

"Jacob? Naturally."

Grace reflected and said flatly, "I never felt less in a party mood."

"Oh, you will be when you dress in Willa's clothes. She was always in a party mood."

The eerie apprehension was descending on her again.

"But you can't want me to do that! You don't like me in Willa's clothes." Slowly she added, "Why?"

"The party is really for me," Polsen explained. "I think it's time I came out of the background and met your friends."

"Not *my* friends," Grace said vehemently.

"Yours, for that night. You will be Willa. Don't you understand?"

"This is intended to be a joke? A sick joke."

"Not necessarily. Unless one particular guest thinks it sick." He looked at Grace anxiously. "Do you think it a good ploy? Better than yours about an abortion."

"Ploy!"

"That was your word."

"It's a *creepy* idea!"

"I thought you'd enjoy it. With your sort of imagination."

Wearing those butterfuly glasses again, and the party pyjamas, and the Balenciaga scent . . .

"Do I have to get my hair dyed yellow?" she asked in utter distaste.

To her surprise Polsen's voice was equally full of distaste.

"No, certainly not. You can wear a wig. Find one the right colour. Find the hairdresser who did Willa's hair, if you can."

8

THE telephone in Willa's flat began to ring just after Grace and Polsen arrived home. Again, Grace's heart gave a great leap of hope. Was it Willa this time?

She realised that she had become innured to disappointment, for she remained quite calm when the caller was identified as Winifred Wright, the middle-aged secretary from the Embassy.

"You're still here, Grace?"

"But of course. I don't intend leaving until I've seen Willa."

"That's what Peter Sinclair said. He thinks you're optimistic."

"Optimistic?"

"Well, perhaps that isn't the right word." Winifred sounded slightly flustered. "I meant that he thinks Willa's more than a bit unreliable. Anyway, since you're here, we'd like to look after you. Can you come out for a meal one evening?"

Had Peter Sinclair asked Winifred to share

the chore of keeping an eye on her? Or was she doing this out of her own kind heart?

"I'd like to. There are a lot of things I want to ask you."

"Such as?" The voice at the other end of the wire was crisp.

"Things puzzling me. Do you know the hairdresser Willa went to, for instance?"

"Yes, I do, but you're not going blonde, are you?"

"Willa seemed to have plenty of success that way. Although one would have thought the Swedes would prefer brunettes, for a change. Winifred, I'm going to give a party. Will you come?"

"But you don't know people here, do you?"

"A few. The rest will be Willa's friends. I thought this could be a sort of wedding party with the bride and groom unfortunately in absentia. But we can drink their health. What a pity that poor Bill Jordan is dead."

For a moment there was a complete silence, then . . .

"Why Bill Jordan?" Winifred asked.

"Wasn't he a special friend of Willa's?"

"I don't think so. He wasn't her type.

He kept to himself rather. He was shy with girls."

"Good looking?"

"Very."

"Then that's it. I can just see Willa winkling him out of his shell. She was extremely good with shy young men."

"He's dead, if that's anything to do with it," Winifred said gruffly.

"What an incongruous remark," Grace said carefully. "What do you mean? Do *you* think Bill Jordan's death was suicide?"

"Why?" Now Winifred's voice was sharp, with an undercurrent of wariness. "Does someone else?"

"I heard a rumour. Do you think he had worries?"

"You mean, was he breaking his heart over Willa? If he was, she deserves strangling. I know she's your cousin and all that but she can be a little bitch."

Grace, feeling her way, had got a more shattering reaction than she had expected.

"That nice young man," Winifred was going on indignantly. "Everyone knew he was unhappy. We all tried to get him to talk, but he wouldn't."

"And so Peter Sinclair had a last attempt?"

"Yes. But he got nothing out of him, although they both got a bit drunk. Bill was the buttoned-up kind. He just went out and had this accident, or whatever it was. Hell, Grace!" Winifred's voice was full of disgust. "I thought we were talking about a party, not a funeral. When's it to be?"

"Saturday—six o'clock. And that hairdresser?"

"A little place called Ingrid on Strandvagen, not far from you. But honestly, what are you trying to do? Be Willa? You don't look the bitchy type to me."

Grace laughed and put down the telephone and looked at Polsen, silent in the corner.

"You got the gist of that?"

"Mostly."

"It seems the rumour is that Willa drove Bill Jordan to his death. That must be why she talked hysterically about murder."

"Then all I can say is that he must have been a remarkably stupid young man. To lose his life for a butterfly like Willa."

Grace frowned in perplexity. "What's wrong with her? She never used to be like that. Thoughtless but not heartless. She was particularly warm-hearted."

"Don't be so upset, Grace. One man,

144

anyway, has found her warm-hearted. She's going to have a baby, remember?"

"Does that indicate a warm heart? Or a trap she's got herself caught in?"

"And could have got out of if she had wanted to. She obviously prefers to keep her baby."

"And her Gustav." Grace pressed her hands to her temples. "This is enough for to-day, Polsen. I'm going to bed. Maybe Willa will be back tomorrow and I won't have to have my hair dyed yellow or have a party that isn't a party, or ask another single question."

But the narrow bed with the curved ends was not a restful one. Charming, but not comfortable. It seemed to close her in too much, as if she were back in her cradle and helpless. It gave her dreams that were claustrophobic and horrible, although she couldn't remember their horror when she woke. Something about being unable to find her way out of the dark forest, and the snow beginning to fall like goose feathers.

The next day, Ingrid's long and pale cynical face with its high crown of blonde hair looked into the mirror above Grace's.

"A rinse, certainly, froken. But not that colour. Not for you. Seriously, I wouldn't

145

recommend it. What about a streak or two of silver? Here and here?"

A thin long-nailed finger poked at Grace's hair.

"You gave my cousin a rinse and it was an enormous success."

"Yes? Do I remember her?"

"Willa Bedford. From the British Embassy."

"*Ja, ja!* I remember." The melancholy face suddenly crumpled up with laughter. "She was a character. I want to make an impact, Ingrid, she used to say. I'm not an Embassy wife who has to be discreet. I'm only a secretary. Who's going to look at me if I don't give them something to look at?"

Was. Used to. The past tense again . . .

The woman's fingers rested on each side of Grace's temples, as she studied Grace's face in the mirror.

"But you don't need to make that sort of impact."

"No, I don't suppose I would be very successful at carrying it off," Grace said resignedly.

"I didn't mean that. I meant that, frankly, you would look terrible. You're the intellectual type, yes?"

"Oh, hell," said Grace.

The hollow laughter came again.

"You don't like to be that? But it's much more distinguished. Now me, I would give anything to look clever. Is it true that Froken Bedford has run off with a man?"

"Is that what you've heard?"

Ingrid had picked up a pair of scissors and begun to snip at Grace's hair.

"*Ja*, I heard that. She told me herself. Give me a special do today, Ingrid, she said. I'm going to be married. Who is the lucky man, I asked, and she said it was a secret, but she called him Gustav."

"Was she happy and excited?" Grace asked.

"Excited, yes. But there were difficulties, she said. She might have to be patient for a while. But it was all going to be wonderful in the end. Now, froken, I suggest a simple casual style—like this, and this."

Grace regarded the work of Ingrid's skilful fingers. She said reluctantly, "I suppose so. But, like Willa, I have an occasion for making an impact. So what I must have is an inexpensive yellow wig."

The long face in the mirror expressed nothing but shock.

"It's for a joke," Grace said defiantly.

147

SHE WENT home with the wig box containing its impossible concoction of nylon curls bouncing on her arm. Four hundred kroners down the drain, she was thinking. Were she and Polsen letting this macabre game they had invented run away with them?

The strange man was halfway down the stairs when she arrived home. She stood at the bottom, waiting for him to complete his descent. Fru Lindstrom's ears were at the alert, for her door opened at that moment and she appeared, clapping her hands as if in surprise and exclaiming, "Captain Morgensson, delay a moment and meet your new neighbour, Froken Asherton."

The cool blue stare, the thick blonde beard that partially concealed pink sensuous lips. Gustav? But no, the nose was a little too long, the forehead too high, the eyes too cool and watchful. Just for a moment, however, Grace had been startled. Was Willa's likeness derived from a vivid momentary impression?

"Willa's cousin, I believe? My aunts talked of you." Captain Morgensson's English was heavily accented. He took her hand in a hard grip. "You called on them, they told me. They enjoyed your visit."

"You're just home from a voyage?" Grace said politely.

"From Greenland. I am glad to get warm again." Captain Morgensson gave a hearty laugh, but his eyes had caught the frosty glitter of the ice packs he had been sailing through. No wonder his stare had made Willa uneasy.

"My name is Axel," he said. "I hope to see more of you, Miss Grace, before I sail again. Now that Willa has jilted me to get herself a husband." He gave another loud laugh in which Fru Lindstrom joined. They both seemed to laugh for the sake of making a noise. As if there must not be any seriousness when the amusing and frivolous Willa was talked about.

Grace swung the wig box on her arm and imitated their gaiety.

"You must come to my party next Saturday, Captain. I'm having a few friends to drink Willa's health."

"Willa will be there!"

Her imagination was running away with her. There couldn't have been such surprise in his voice. As if he had reason to know Willa's presence would be an impossibility.

"Who knows? She'll turn up when she

149

turns up. But in the meantime we can drink her health. Do come if you can. Bring your aunts, too."

"Thank you, Miss Grace. For my aunts I can't promise, but for myself I will be delighted to come."

"That's marvellous. Six o'clock, Saturday. I'll see you then."

She knew that his inquisitive stare was following her up the stairs, but it was quite impossible to guess what he was thinking. Nothing, but nothing, got any clearer. Could she hope for anything better when she met the last man mentioned in Willa's diary? Jacob, the Baron von Sturpe, the elegant Ebba's husband. That was, if the von Sturpes agreed to come to her party.

At home she would never have had the temerity to give a party like this. There was no doubt that in an uncanny way she was taking on some of Willa's haphazard, gay but curiously fatalistic personality. She studied the telephone directory, and began to make confident telephone calls. She was quite certain of acceptances. Most people would come out of curiosity. But she had an intuition that there would be one or two who had no curiosity, only that watchfulness she had encountered already.

Well, she and Polsen could be watchful, too.

The surprised, but cordial voice of the Countess von Sturpe, the more guarded voice of Doctor Sven Backe who would be delighted to come and bring his sister Ulrika, Winifred Wright, and other friends of Willa's from the Embassy, the Thompsons and the Hendersons whom Grace had met at Peter Sinclair's party, the frail voice of Miss Anna Morgensson accepting with pleasure for herself and her sister, and her nephew Axel, fortuitously home at this time. The last call Grace made was to the Sinclairs. Kate answered. Her voice was unbelieving.

"A party! At this time!"

She spoke as if the time should be one for mourning. She seemed to be outdoing the Swedes in their talent for melancholy. It couldn't be much fun for her husband.

"What's wrong with this time?"

"But for Willa, when she isn't even here! You're beginning to behave exactly like her, Grace."

"How?" Grace asked interestedly.

"Doing these offbeat things. A party for someone who has gone."

"But not forever. She may even be back to

take part in it. Anyway, you and Peter can come, can't you?"

"I'll have to confirm it with Peter. He keeps his diary in his office. I never know what we're doing." The faintly whining voice was the old Kate. "And Georgy has come down with a temperature. If Alexander gets it, too, I'll have to stay home."

"Oh, I'm sorry."

"Yes, it couldn't be at a more awkward time. I'm supposed to go to a tea party at the Residence this afternoon."

"Then go. I'll come out and stay with the children."

"Grace! Would you?"

"Of course. I'd like to."

"Really—you are nice. Willa was good-natured like that, too."

"You've already told me I'm like her. I didn't think you meant it as a compliment."

Kate gave an uneasy laugh. "You'd better not take any notice of me. I'm a bit mixed-up. And I so hate this place. It wasn't so bad until Bill's death. I can't seem to get over that. Not that he was a very close friend. Just that it was so sad."

"Is that why you got prejudiced against Willa?" Grace asked.

"Willa! Oh, goodness, no. I don't think she had anything to do with it."

"Winifred Wright thought she had."

"I know there were rumours. But Peter wouldn't pay any attention to them. He said Bill knew the type of girl Willa was, and wouldn't have taken her seriously."

"Well, someone apparently has," Grace said lightly.

"Has what?"

"Taken Willa seriously."

There was a long pause.

"Or it could be the other way round," Kate said slowly, at last. "Have you thought of that, Grace? That Willa has taken someone seriously."

"You mean, someone who isn't serious about her?"

"It would only be what she deserved, wouldn't it?"

JUST BEFORE Grace was ready to leave for the Sinclairs at four o'clock as she had promised, Kate was on the telephone again.

"Grace, I promised to pick up Joyce Thompson so I'll have to leave now. The children will be all right until you arrive, but come as soon as you can, will you? Alexander will let you in. And do make Georgy stay in bed. She's being very tiresome. She'll probably behave better for you than she does for me. I won't be more than a couple of hours. Have a drink with Peter if he's home before me."

Half an hour later Alexander opened the door to Grace's ring. He looked wide-eyed and important.

"Georgy says she wants to see you immediately."

"Does she? Can she give me time to take my coat off? How are you, Alexander?"

"I've been answering the telephone, but Georgy wouldn't let me talk. She isn't fair. She says I'm too little to take important messages."

Grace hung up her coat and ruffled the little boy's hair affectionately.

"Sounds just like a girl, doesn't she? Who was the important message from?"

"Willa," said Alexander.

Grace stared at the innocent face. "Willa!"

Alexander nodded, pouting. "And I wanted to ask her about the elks in the forest."

Grace raced upstairs.

"Georgy! Georgy, is it true you were just talking to Willa?"

Georgy was lying back on her pillows, flushed and frowning.

"Don't speak so loudly, Grace. I have a headache."

"Alexander says Willa was on the telephone just now. Is it true?"

"Yes. I just talked to her. I had to go into Mummy's and Daddy's room to answer the telephone and now I feel dizzy."

"But what did she *say*?"

"Just to tell Daddy to come and rescue her. She was tired of the forest and the rain dripping on the roof."

The rain dripping on the roof is driving me mad . . .

"Georgy, you're making this up."

Georgy opened hurt eyes.

"I am not. It was Willa. Ask Alexander."

"He says you wouldn't let him talk to her."

"No, he's too little. Daddy says he isn't allowed to take messages, he gets them wrong."

Grace sat on the side of the bed. She laid her hand on the child's hot forehead.

"Don't you think you might, too, when you're running a temperature? You must have imagined that was Willa. She wouldn't say such an extraordinary thing. What does

155

your father have to rescue her from?"

"The elks, of course," said Alexander in the doorway. "She's frightened of elks. Like I is."

Georgy lay with closed eyes, saying wearily, "She only said Daddy wasn't to shoot them because she didn't like blood. Grace, will you read to us?"

"Georgy—"

"I'm really too sick to talk any more."

"If you could get up to answer the telephone, you can manage to answer questions. Or were you having a dream? Fever makes you dream."

"In the night I had to call for Mummy. I had a nightmare."

"So Willa wasn't on the telephone at all?"

"It was a lady," said Alexander doubtfully.

"But there was nothing about elks in the forest?"

Georgy opened fever-bright eyes.

"It was Alexander who made that up. Willa only said about the rain dripping."

Grace looked at the window as raindrops spattered against the glass. The driving grey clouds had lowered. It was dark, and time to draw the curtains, to shut out the night, to disperse a sick child's fancy.

If it were a fancy . . .

But she had to tell the strange little episode to Peter and Kate who eventually came in within minutes of each other. She related it half flippantly, having almost convinced herself that it hadn't happened. There was a moment of silence. Peter staring, Kate giving an unguarded look as stunned and fearful as the children's when they talked of their nightmare elks.

"And I was to rescue her!" Peter said, after that moment of surprise or shock or whatever it had been. "What an extraordinary imagination those kids have."

"I'll go and ask Georgy myself," Kate exclaimed.

"She's asleep," Grace said. "She's very flushed. I think her temperature may be higher."

"Send for the doctor," said Peter impatiently. "You can't mess around with these things. The child's obviously delirious."

"There probably was a telephone call," Grace said reasonably. "But whether it was from Willa is another matter."

Kate, halfway up the stairs, turned a still face.

"If it was her she can ring again. Can't she?"

If she was asking Peter that question, he chose to ignore it.

"Stuff and nonsense. The kids hear too many fairy stories. I suppose I'm to rescue Willa from her wicked seducer on my white charger."

"Batman would be better, dear. You might as well be up to date."

Kate's sad ironical voice lingered in Grace's ears after she had gone home. She banged on the ceiling to bring Polsen down, and once more related the story.

"It's the bit about the rain that disturbs me. Don't you remember Willa writing in her diary that the rain on the roof was driving her mad? The children didn't know that, did they? So why should Georgy talk about rain?"

"Because it is raining and she could hear it. I expect children say the first thing that comes into their heads."

Grace listened to the prickling of the wind-driven showers on her own windows. The sound was melancholy enough in the city, but in the forest, on the iron roof of one of those claustrophobic cottages, it must be infinitely depressing.

"I can't help feeling Willa's in a cottage in the forest. But whether she's a prisoner—"

"With a telephone?"

"Maybe Gustav left her alone for a few minutes."

Polsen put back his head and gave his deep tolerant laugh.

"Now who's being fanciful? And you haven't even Georgy's excuse of a high temperature."

"Polsen, don't laugh at me. I think it's almost time Willa was reported as missing. Shouldn't I go to the police, or to the British Ambassador at least?"

Polsen stopped laughing.

"Not yet. Even the Swedish police are sentimental enough not to want to pursue an eloping bride. And your ambassador probably knows all he wants to know about it already."

"What do you mean by not yet?" Grace asked tensely.

"Not till after your party. That may prove to be more enlightening than you expect. Now what about a schnapps? Willa's old potato drink. She said that, too. She didn't always talk about rain."

Polsen, as always, was comforting, taking

159

the melodrama out of the situation, but not denying the mystery. He never made her feel foolish, yet succeeded in reducing her fears to the bearable.

All the same, he admitted, it was a pity she hadn't arrived at the Sinclairs a few minutes earlier and had spoken to the mysterious caller herself. It could well have been Willa in a spot of bother with her passport or marriage licence. Who better to call than Peter Sinclair in that event?

"Which means she'll call again," Grace said, reassured at last. She remembered then to tell Polsen about her meeting with Captain Axel Morgensson that morning. She understood now what Willa meant about him. "He has the most penetrating stare. He tries to look inside your head. He would see nothing but a muddle inside mine at present. Polsen, you're not going? Don't leave me alone. I rather hate being alone. Listening to that dreary wind. Thinking."

Polsen gave his slow gratified smile.

"Actually I was going to suggest you have supper with me. You haven't seen my studio. You might like to see my paintings. We could talk of something else than Willa who has had more than her share of attention."

"Polsen, you don't have to do that much."

"Don't be so diffident. Be like Willa. She would say, 'And about time, too.' "

"You said we wouldn't talk about Willa."

"So I did. I apologise."

"But if she did make that telephone call it means she's alive," Grace burst out, and then couldn't think what had made her say such a thing. Of course Willa was alive. In spite of her irresponsible ways she was far too vital a person to die.

The top floor studio, a low-ceilinged long room warmed by an enormous porcelain stove, and in a state of extraordinary untidiness, was full of strange comfort. Books and paintings, after all, were the best furnishings a room could have, even if piled haphazardly all over the place. There was also an old-fashioned rocking chair, a large faded wool rug, tables and chairs piled with the overflowing books, an easel with a half-finished painting, and a portrait of a child, a tow-headed boy, propped on the mantelpiece.

Polsen was watching Grace. His expression was half-pleased, half-anxious.

"You're not getting an uncontrollable urge to tidy me up?"

"No."

"You don't mind the muddle?"

"It's you, Polsen. Why should I want to alter you? Is that your son?"

"Yes."

"I saw him with you the other day. I waved but you didn't see me."

"I expect we were discussing some highly important subject."

"You're good friends, aren't you?"

"Of course."

"But not good enough to want to live with his mother?"

"No." His voice had become withdrawn, colder than she had heard it. "That's a matter of human dignity. I would have expected you to understand."

"I do. Except that if you and Magnus are so close, perhaps you could put up with a little indignity. I mean, to have more than just Sundays."

"Some people could," he said distantly. "Not me."

She wanted to pursue the subject, probing his wound, testing his reaction to her interest. But before she could ask another question he said in his usual mild voice, "You're being female, Grace. That's all right, but not about this subject. Now you would look nice in my rocking chair. I'll give you a drink and then I must begin to cook if we're to eat tonight."

A little later he called from the kitchen, "Do you mind the wind up here? It sounds louder than in your place."

It did sound louder, wild and forlorn like the far-off howl of wolves. Yet now it gave Grace nothing but a feeling of tranquillity. She was beginning to think she might be a little, gently, in love with Polsen. And if she were that tow-headed boy in the portrait would be her enemy.

But perhaps this latest feat of imagination came from weariness and the schnapps going to her head. A child could never be an enemy.

"No," she said. "I don't mind the wind up here. Perhaps it will begin to snow."

9

THEY arrived together, the two people she had not met, the Baron von Sturpe, and Ulrika Backe, sister of Sven. The Baroness Ebba and Doctor Sven Backe were there, too, of course. They had followed one another, Sven said, the Baron's Mercedes hard on the tail of his little Volvo.

"We could have eaten the Volvo up," Ebba said in her husky voice. "But we played cat and mouse. Grace, my dear, how nice of you to ask us to your party. You haven't met my husband. Jacob, this is Miss Grace Asherton. I think English names are delightful, so much prettier than Swedish ones."

The Baron gave a small correct bow. To Grace's surprise, he was a small, almost elderly man, towered over by his tall wife. He had grey hair, mild eyes, a deprecating smile, and quite definitely was not the kind who would make an impression on Willa who liked more flamboyant types. Except perhaps for his title or his money, both of which

164

possessions had probably caught the spectacular Ebba for him.

One would have thought Sven Backe, with his melancholy good looks, would have made a more suitable partner for Ebba, and Ulrika, the square-set unsmiling sister could have stood at the Baron's side.

Look at me changing partners already, Grace said to herself. The Swedes were quite capable of doing that for themselves.

"So you are still enjoying Stockholm," Sven Backe said, looking at her with dark nervous eyes. She hadn't noticed their nervousness the other day in his surgery. Perhaps he didn't like parties. Perhaps his sister inhibited him. She stood determinedly close to him. Or perhaps she was nervous, too, in her black wool dress cut too high round her short thick neck. She would realise her lack of elegance beside Ebba in a long silvery dress that shimmered in the candlelight. Her big pale eyes had taken on the same cool silver colour.

Polsen had said there must be dozens of candles. They were festive, intimate, kind to women's complexions, they added warmth to the room. Willa's parties had always been candlelit.

But the wavering flames seemed to make the faces waver, too, and become most shadowy when one wanted most to read their expressions. Captain Axel Morgensson meeting Ebba, giving her his intense stare. Peter Sinclair greeting Sven Backe too heartily, as if they were old friends, and yet having to be introduced to the dour Ulrika. Polsen being unusually attentive to Kate Sinclair, Winifred Wright talking too fast and too archly to the Baron von Sturpe who surely was a man on whom archness would be wasted. Axel's old aunts sitting on Willa's lush velvet-cushioned couch and smiling and nodding pleasantly as if they heard every word that was being said.

"Great party, Grace," said Nigel Thompson. "You have as much talent as Willa."

"Did you used to come to her parties?"

"Sure. So did most people here. You've certainly rounded up the old mob."

"I thought she would like it. It's time to drink her health. And Gustav's."

"The mysterious Gustav."

"Does no one have a clue who he is? It's incredible. You all knew Willa."

Joyce Thompson, Nigel's wife, had joined them.

"Not that well, Grace. She was a terrible

exhibitionist. She always had to make an entrance. People like that hide their real selves, don't you think? Hide their lovers, too, obviously."

"But she was bloody good fun," said Nigel.

Grace put her glass down thoughtfully. An entrance. That was her cue.

She caught Polsen's eye across the room. He'd deliberately begun blowing out candles until there were only a dozen or so left burning. Then he began going the rounds, filling up everyone's glass.

"We're going to drink to Willa and Gustav."

"But it's so dark," exclaimed Miss Anna Morgensson.

"Too dark?" Grace, from the bedroom, heard him saying courteously. "That's for atmosphere. A tribute to Willa. She liked atmosphere, sensation, mystery."

"You sound a bit valedictory, old man," said Nigel Thompson.

Grace, behind the bedroom door, struggling with the slippery silk pyjama suit, her fingers trembling too much for speed, heard Peter Sinclair observe, "Yes, she liked mystery a bit too much for the comfort of Her Majesty's Government. We're vetting our typists more carefully now. Aren't we, Winifred?"

"We're all going to be too staid for words," Winifred complained. "I'm thinking of applying for a transfer to the Far East."

The wig wouldn't fit securely. It would tumble off, like a guillotined head, like a sunflower blasted by frost.

But it would stay on long enough. And the dark butterfly-shaped glasses and the long cigarette holder, and the tottery high heels, and the dash of Balenciaga perfume.

It was ridiculous, really. Did Willa realise how nineteen thirty-ish she had been?

But this was 1969, bleak, cold, devious, and now was the moment.

She flung open the door, slipped into the darkened living room, and cried gaily, "*Voilà!*"

Someone screamed. She didn't know whom. She thought it was one of the old ladies, Miss Anna or Miss Katerina. It couldn't have been the sophisticated self-controlled Ebba whose face, in the dim light, had a candle-white pallor. Then Winifred Wright began to laugh hysterically, and exclaim, "Willa! You damn fool! You've scared us all to death."

"And your husband?" That was Captain Morgensson in his guttural voice. "Is he here, also?"

Grace couldn't keep it up. She was trembling too violently. She felt terrible, like a skeleton ejected from its dark safe cupboard after too many years. She made a shaky gesture towards Polsen, and he crossed over to her and with the air of a magician lifted the wig from her head.

"A joke," he said pleasantly. "A wonderful performance, Grace. Applause for Grace, please!"

Someone began uncertainly to clap, then stopped.

"Take off those damned glasses," came Peter Sinclair's voice angrily in Grace's ear, and at the same time there was a gentle slither of someone subsiding slowly to the floor.

When everyone had stepped back and more candles had been lit it was discovered that the person who had been overcome was Kate Sinclair.

She was already trying to sit up. Ebba knelt beside her. "A glass of water," she said. Polsen went to get it, and Grace, somewhat remorsefully pushing her way to Kate's side, was put aside by Peter who suddenly seemed

169

to realise that it was his wife who had been stricken.

"Joke, Kate," he said loudly. "Didn't you hear?"

Kate pushed the hair back from her pallid forehead.

"I'm sorry," she muttered, "the candles were too hot. That's all."

She recovered sufficiently to sit in a chair, but presently Peter said he had better take her home. She was probably coming down with the bug the children had. He wiped his own forehead which was shiny with perspiration.

But everyone looked hot. Even Ebba had spots of colour on her high cheekbones, giving her face an attractive look of animation. She was very solicitous of Kate. Grace wouldn't have thought she possessed such concern. Not for another woman, anyway.

Polsen had opened a window to let a stream of cold night air into the overheated room. Grace thought he would be chagrined that their experiment had been ruined by Kate's behaviour, but he looked as imperturbable as ever. And after all, when she came to think of it, there had been that split second reaction of surprise and shock. Distinct shock. Kate's collapse may have come as a welcome diversion. Certainly the tension had gone out of the atmosphere once the lights were switched on and the remaining candles blown out. The room had a smell of candle smoke. The normal party noise was beginning again.

"Grace, that was a horrid joke," Kate murmured plaintively, as Peter helped her into her coat.

"Why horrid? Didn't you want to see Willa? Didn't anyone want to see her?"

Grace spoke on a sudden belligerent note, turning to the room at large.

"Don't be silly, Grace," came Ebba's low controlled voice. "We'd all adore to see her. I only don't understand why you had to play that charade. As if there were a mystery or something."

"Isn't there a mystery?"

"Well, darling, I expect you know your cousin better than any of us here. If she's acting out of context—how do you say that?"

"Out of character," supplied Sven Backe.

"That's right. How clever of you, Sven. Well, we just wouldn't know about that, would we? I, anyway, didn't know Willa well enough."

"Eloping isn't a thing a girl does every day," observed Axel. "Not even Miss Willa."

171

"Yes, Grace, have you known her manner of eloping in the past?" Peter Sinclair said, his arm round his wife, the facetiousness back in his voice. "We English let our lives be ruled by precedent."

"I don't care how you rationalise it," Grace said stubbornly. "To me there is a mystery. And I won't be satisfied until I get to the bottom of it."

She could do a little outstaring herself, even with Axel Morgensson. But this was foolish. These were her guests, not her enemies. Why did that little flutter come over her that they all hated her? Even Winifred Wright, with her puzzled slightly outraged expression. Letting the side down, was she?

"Let's all have another drink," came Polsen's calm voice.

"Such a draught, all at once," complained Miss Anna Morgensson.

Then Fru Lindstrom's jolly laugh restored normality.

"But what an actress you are, Froken Asherton. I really believed you were Froken Bedford. Everyone did."

Everyone? Then why that sudden moment of petrified shock, as if Willa's appearance was such an astonishing, even unwelcome thing?

"It's worse than before," Grace murmured to Polsen pouring drinks in the kitchen.

"What?"

"The mystery."

"Repercussions," said Polsen obscurely.

"What do you mean?"

"How many drinks is that? Enough? We must wait for the repercussions."

"Tonight?" Grace's heart was jumping nervously again.

"Who knows? Come along. You're neglecting your guests."

And the first repercussion, if it were one, happened even sooner than could have been expected.

"Grace, would you come and spend next weekend with us?" Ebba asked. "Have you visited an old Swedish house?"

"Only Gripsholm castle."

"Ours isn't exactly a castle, but it's early eighteenth century. I think you'll find it interesting. Do come."

"I'd love to," Grace said with a private feeling of recklessness that should not accompany an acceptance of an invitation to a weekend in the country.

"Marvellous. We're not far from Sigtuna. Sven and Ulrika might come over for dinner. Unless you want to be quiet."

"I don't want to be quiet," said Grace. "Why?"

"I can't imagine why I said that. Of course you don't. We might even have a party."

AFTERWARDS, Grace wished Ebba had included Polsen in her invitation. But why should she, any more than she should include Axel, or any of the Embassy people? She wondered, too, if Willa had ever spent a weekend with the Baron and Baroness, but that she could discover later.

Polsen gave her his inscrutable look when she told him of this development.

"Should I have accepted?"

"Of course. Why not?"

"I wish you had been asked, too."

"Me? The dull professor?"

"I'm not exactly scintillating myself. I expect Ebba is just thinking she ought to be hospitable to a visitor to her country."

"Get her to take you to Uppsala. There's a fine university there. And a cathedral."

"You could have done that," said Grace. "I would have been happier with you."

"Then all right. Save it for me. Go driving in the forest instead."

"The forest?"

"There's miles of forest round the von Sturpe estate. And the lake, of course. Sigtuna is pretty. But it's the wrong time of year."

"I hope it won't be raining." Grace repressed a shiver. "I don't really want to go. I haven't the right sort of clothes."

"Borrow Willa's."

"Yes, I suppose I could. She wouldn't mind. I can leave a note of explanation in case she comes back while I am away."

THIS, HOWEVER, proved to be unnecessary, for two days later the letter from Willa arrived.

It was addressed to Grace in England and had been readdressed by Grace's father. The postmark was too blurred to read, but the date on the letter, which Grace unfolded with fingers that shook ridiculously, was exactly a week ago.

There was no address.

Dear Grace,

You must be wondering why I haven't written sooner, but Gustav and I are having a

spot of bother. Gustav was too optimistic about a tiresome divorce he has to get, did I tell you? It has been delayed, so I'm having to wait a while to be made an honest woman. It won't be too long, but it's a bit maddening and depressing. I'm beginning to show, as they say. But unless something absolutely unforeseen happens we'll get to the altar in time. Gustav is holding my hand, bless him. Don't worry about me. I'll be seeing you long before I make you an aunt. No, you'll be a second cousin, won't you? Doesn't matter. Just come to Sweden and see the little beast.
All love, Wilhelmina.

"There it is!" Grace said to Polsen, pointing with her still trembling finger. "Wilhelmina! Again. So she *is* in trouble."

"Yes. She must be. No divorce, no husband."

"Not just that. Willa would take a situation like that in her stride. It wouldn't be something she had to send me a cry for help about."

"Something more serious," Polsen said thoughtfully. It was a statement rather than a question.

Grace nodded, her lips dry. She had only

been apprehensive before, she realised. Now she was frightened.

Polsen held the envelope up to the light, studying the blotted postmark.

"Uppsala," he said, at length.

"Are you sure?"

"Yes. Look. Here's the U, and there the tails of the two P's. An A at the end. It shouldn't be too difficult to find Willa there. A pregnant English girl in a small university town would be fairly visible. Why are you looking so critical?"

"A letter posted in Uppsala doesn't need to mean she's there. She could still be in that cottage in the forest."

"And only came to town to post the letter and telephone the Sinclairs?"

"Not even that," said Grace unhappily. "I'm certain Gustav made her write this letter, and then took it himself to post it. He's seen that she's written in her usual style, but he still doesn't know about her secret signature. Her S.O.S. to me, who she thinks is in England. What does she imagine I can do there, when I can't even do anything here?"

Polsen looked at her admiringly.

"What a brain you have, Grace. You'll be a great writer."

"Never mind that—"

"I was going to say that now I'll do some guessing. Willa doesn't know you're in Stockholm, but Gustav does. Right? He's getting a little disturbed at the way you're behaving, so he's had Willa write this letter, cleverly addressed to England, knowing it would be sent on to you here, and hoping it would put your mind at rest."

"It's done the very opposite!"

"But only because of the private signature, which Gustav doesn't know about. All criminals make some small but dangerous mistake."

"Criminals!"

"He is hardly an honest man. Is he?"

"Oh, Polsen!" Grace pressed her hands to her temples in despair. "What are we to do now? Has this horrible man got Willa hidden away until somehow he makes her get rid of the baby?"

"Too simple. No one would go to those lengths for something that could be done comparatively easily. It must be more than that. I'm sorry. But I have to say I am now a little alarmed."

"Me, too."

"There was never another telephone call to the Sinclairs?"

"Kate says not. She didn't find out who that caller was. She thinks the children made it up."

"Then let us reflect. You had better go to the von Sturpes this weekend, as planned."

"Must I?"

"It's better, I think. Just keep your eyes and ears open. It will be all right. You'll enjoy it. Try to get invited to the Backes, too."

Grace's face was harrowed as she thought of the ordeal ahead. It was an ordeal in spite of Polsen's calm way of assuming it would be enjoyable. Ebba with her intimidating assurance and sophistication, and her eighteenth-century house full, no doubt, of dark stairways and old portraits, the Strindberg house of the Backes, with Mama, Papa, and the dour sister Ulrika. And always the gloomy forest and the steely shine of the lake, and the wind howling, and the sky heavy with snow that refused to fall.

"Ugh!" Grace was shivering again. "What a country this is. Keep this place warm for me, Polsen."

"I'll be doing more than that." His hand rested briefly, she fancied affectionately, on her head. "While you're enjoying your baronial dinner parties."

But he wouldn't say what it was he would be doing, and once again she was reluctantly compelled to believe that he suspected, or knew, more than he intended to tell her.

10

EVERYONE but Polsen watched Grace leave with Ebba who had arrived in her white Mercedes. Was it chance that caught Captain Morgensson hurrying down the stairs with a canvas bag slung over his shoulder at that precise moment? His aunts were leaning over the stair-rail waving to him, and saying something in Swedish. When Grace appeared they called "*Farval*" to her, too, and hoped she would have a nice time.

"Is your ship sailing?" Grace asked Captain Morgensson who had stood back politely to let her pass.

"*Ja!* Shortly. I will be seeing you when I return again, I hope." His bleak eyes held a stirring of warmth. Merely sensual, Grace thought. Merely his automatic reaction to a woman.

Fru Lindstrom, as was to be expected, was in the hall, being deferential to Ebba. Grace got included in this distasteful servility.

"Ah, Froken Asherton, how fortunate you

are, a beautiful drive, a weekend in the country." Her hearty laugh rang in Grace's ears as she followed Ebba outdoors. It was useless to wish that Polsen, also, was joining in this cosy farewell. But he had gone out very early. She had heard his firm footsteps going down the stairs before she was up. She had thought he might be back before she left, but he had not been, and she was unreasonably disappointed. If he hadn't waited to say goodbye, he might at least have told her where he was going. She was getting as inquisitive as Fru Lindstrom.

Ebba, as svelte as ever in a high-necked sweater and a suede jacket, her ashen hair tied back with a black velvet ribbon, was friendly enough in her cool off-hand way.

"We'll be home in good time for lunch. Then you can see over the house. Are you interested in architecture? Swedish history?"

"Everything."

"Yes, I suppose a writer has to have a curious mind."

Was there an underlying meaning in that remark? She was getting too suspicious. Ebba's profile was pure and calm.

"I have a very curious mind," Grace answered.

"Then use it on the Backes who have invited us to tea this afternoon. There's a family that's turned in on itself. Such a pity. Sven could be so charming if he weren't so inhibited. Tomorrow the Sinclairs and the Backes are all coming for the day. Jacob likes to go shooting with Peter and Sven. We women can have a lazy time."

"Shooting elks?" asked Grace.

"Did I hear apprehension in your voice? You're thinking of that poor young man, Bill Jordan. It's time that was forgotten. There are hunting accidents every year. So are there car accidents, and other unfortunate things. It does no one any good to brood on them. Look at Kate. She lets simply everything get her down. I have no time for neurotic women, especially when they become such a liability on their husbands. If Kate isn't careful she'll ruin Peter's job for him, and that would be a great pity. He's so clever and able. Don't you agree?"

"I don't really know him well enough. I feel sorry for Kate, but she is pretty limp. Still, she might have been like Willa, and I suppose that would have been worse."

"How?" There was a sharp inflection in Ebba's voice.

"Flirting with everyone. Starting scandals. I've had the feeling ever since I've been here that every man I've met could tell me more about Willa than he has done."

Ebba gave her low amused laugh.

"Even my husband? Well, you may be right. She was a foolish creature, but one had to admire her vitality. Men always like vitality, don't they? What about your Polsen?"

"He's not mine!"

"Am I wrong? I thought he was quite possessive. Sweet, too, if you like that type. Do you know anything about him, except what he wants you to think? The gentle bumbling professor? Perhaps not so bumbling if the truth were known. I expect he has a good brain?"

She was being cross-examined, Grace realised, and took satisfaction in answering non-committally, "I wouldn't know. We haven't discussed intellectual subjects."

"What do you talk about?" Ebba asked.

"Willa, mostly."

"Good gracious! What a thing! Another woman! Was that bad joke you played at your party his idea?"

"Partly. We thought it would liven up things."

"And it fell flat," said Ebba. "Like Kate." She gave a short laugh. "You ought to know, Grace, that we're all a little bored with the subject of Willa. I'll tell you a little secret. We rather hope she won't turn up again, even with a husband. She is a very tiresome young woman."

"Well, she won't be turning up immediately," Grace said deliberately, watching Ebba's face, which instantly showed all the surprise she could have expected.

"Why? Have you heard from her?"

"Yes, I had a letter. It was sent on to me from England."

"Well, for goodness sake, Grace, you are a secretive person. Why didn't you tell me at once?"

"Even though you're bored with the subject?"

"I'm not bored with real facts. Have you some, at last?"

When Grace had related the contents of Willa's letter, Ebba lifted her handsome head and laughed with the greatest amusement.

"Oh, dear! Forgive me, Grace. But this is exactly what Willa deserves. It won't do her any harm at all. When one thinks of her own behaviour—"

"Are you thinking of Bill Jordan?" Grace interrupted.

"Not only him. She really was a little tramp. You have more or less said so yourself. I think Gustav, whoever he is, is the one to be pitied for having this problem."

"It is his baby," Grace pointed out.

"Oh, that. Such an old-fashioned way to blackmail a man."

Ebba's mind was a cold analytical one. Grace wondered if it ever held warmth and affection, even for her quiet husband. She must have found the untidiness of Willa's life very distasteful, although why it should have affected her was a little puzzling. Unless Willa had made a pass at the quiet Jacob. There did seem something personal in Ebba's satisfaction at Willa's predicament.

Sven, Axel, Jacob, Gustav . . .

"Did Willa ever stay with you?" Grace asked curiously.

"She visited us for a day. She came with the Sinclairs when she was staying in their cottage. Peter and Jacob went out shooting, and took her with them. I never invited her for a weekend. We weren't on those terms of friendship."

Are we? Grace wondered silently.

186

"You're so different from your cousin," Ebba answered for her. "Everyone notices that."

The road ran through the yellow, amber and dark green landscape. Cold grey turrets of clouds hung on the horizon. The ploughed fields, turning the earth up to the sky, looked sodden and sour. A row of sunflowers, their vibrant yellow vanished, hung blackened withered heads, against a roadside cottage. Like Willa with her canary yellow head? Grace wondered involuntarily. Was it hanging withered and forlorn, too?

Ebba slowed down and turned into a narrow rutted road, bordered with birches. It ran in a straight line to a mansion a mile in the distance.

"Home," said Ebba.

It was a handsome house, pineapple-coloured with dark brown facings. A long flight of steps led up to the front door. There were eagles' heads on the balustrades, and a long stretch of lawn with formal gardens on either side of the house. There would be peacocks, Grace thought fancifully. Or pet eagles. It was the sort of place.

The door opened and Jacob stood on the

steps holding out his hand and smiling in his courteous way.

"Welcome, Grace," he said.

He looked older by daylight, his skin drawn over delicate bones, his complexion pallid, his eyes the washed blue of the wintry sky. At least twenty years older than his wife, Grace calculated. Perhaps more. And whatever Ebba might once have felt for him, besides her desire for his title and his handsome house, had clearly dwindled, for now she swept past him into the large square dark-panelled hall, only saying over her shoulder, "We could do with drinks. Come by the fire, Grace. How do you like our baronial hall? One day I'm going to get rid of all this gloomy panelling. I want everything white and gold, like a French château. Jacob says how would his trophies look with that background? But I intend to get rid of the trophies, too."

This seemed to be a long-standing argument, for Jacob, pouring drinks at a vast mahogany sideboard, said good-humouredly, "And the family portraits, don't forget, my darling."

The trophies were elks' and boars' heads, flanked by splendidly barbaric swords and ancient pistols. Grace was inclined to agree with Ebba about them. But the portraits, hanging in an impressive line down the curving staircase and in the shadows of the landing above, looked decorative and colourful. She wondered if Ebba resented Jacob's ancestors because she had none of any importance herself.

"The portraits, too," Ebba agreed. "I'm tired of being examined by all those critical eyes every time I go up or downstairs. When I first came here I thought I would never get used to their disapproval. I thought they used to dislike me because I was young, but then I realised it was because I was alive. So simple, isn't it? Jacob, I'm only teasing. I promise not to get rid of them until—"

"I also am dead?"

"That's exactly what I was going to say, but you make it sound so bad," Ebba grumbled in her husky voice. "And I'll only put them in the attics. With the ghosts of all our vanished servants. These big houses are no joke nowadays. I do a great deal of the work myself. Is it like that in England, Grace?"

"Exactly the same."

"Well, I suppose it's good for lazy

women." Ebba's long elegant hands held out to the fire didn't look as if they were ever occupied with anything more strenuous than a little needlework, but that could be misleading. She probably kept a battery of beauty preparations. She was a curious person, off-hand, blasé, a little cruel to her quiet husband, amusing, witty, fascinating to look at, heartless perhaps, but totally un-relaxed, her restless bones on wires. Why? From discontentment with an elderly dull husband? A traditional house full of disap-proving ancestors? Life in the country? Lack of children? No, that last would be the baron's tragedy, not hers.

And here she went again, putting people into words, dissecting, rationalising. Grace took the glass of sherry from Jacob, and remembered her manners enough to wait for his formal "*Skol*" to her before she drank. She was going to find her visit highly interesting. After all, it wasn't essential to enjoy it.

"Don't imagine you hear things in the attics in the night," Ebba said later, in the large guest room with the curtained four-poster bed. "They're all empty. But the floors creak, especially as it gets colder. The frost gets in. It's too expensive to keep unused rooms heated."

"The queen in the attic," Grace murmured.

"What?"

"Only something Polsen told me about the Haga pavilion. King Gustav used to keep his queen in the attic."

Ebba's eyes took on a curious smoky look when she was interested.

"You're not also thinking of Willa's Gustav, I hope. I should hardly think he has her under lock and key."

"No, hardly," Grace agreed.

"Well, I assure you these attics really are empty, except for all the pieces of impossibly ugly old Swedish furniture I've had put out of sight."

"Aren't you Swedish?" Grace asked, on an intuition.

"Why do you ask that?"

"You speak about Swedish things as if they were foreign."

Ebba gave a faint smile.

"You're very observant, Grace. No, I'm not Swedish, I'm German. But from a long time ago. I was an actress and came here with a touring company when I was eighteen and never went home again. That was twenty years ago. I still talk of some Swedish things disparagingly, I'm afraid. No wonder my husband is disgusted with me. But one has to be honest, hasn't one?"

Honest? Was that a word one could apply to the Baroness von Sturpe? It was too early yet to decide.

At luncheon, with Ebba and Jacob facing each other from opposite ends of a long table, and Grace islanded in the middle, Ebba suddenly said,

"Oh, I forgot to tell you, Jacob, Grace has heard from the bride. Or the hopeful bride."

"Willa?" Jacob's voice was full of an animation Grace hadn't heard before. He seemed pleased. His eyes had brightened. She had a feeling of shock. So Jacob, also, in spite of his sedate age, joined the list of Willa's admirers. She found it difficult to believe. Except that his wife's coolness, with that underlying tendency to cruelty, might well have turned him to someone as spontaneously warm-hearted as Willa.

"She's got divorce problems," Ebba drawled.

"Already!"

"No, it's Gustav who has the divorce

problems," Grace explained. "It sounds a bit messy, but there doesn't seem to be anything anyone can do, especially since she's so mysterious as to where she is."

"Well, I'm glad to hear she's all right," Jacob said, still with that air of relief.

"Good gracious, did you think she had come to a bad end?" Ebba said amusedly.

Ebba made the same remark, in her lightly sarcastic voice, to the Backes later that day.

Even after such a short time, Grace had been glad to leave the big pineapple-coloured house with its desolate views. Her bedroom windows looked over the forest less than a hundred yards away, other windows over the autumn-stripped garden, and the distant lake, its water black in the fading light. It was all too quiet, too brooding.

Alone in her room she had already imagined she heard the nocturnal creakings in the attics. She had never been stupidly nervous like this before. It was ridiculous, but she wanted to cry.

That was it. She kept imagining Willa's lonely queen crying silently, hour by hour, in her small high prison.

Really, this country with its threat of winter, darkness, snow, was affecting her mind. She was getting worse than Kate Sinclair, and that was saying something.

She missed Polsen. And Willa's letter, which had been such a relief at first was weighing on her like those brooding snow-clouds. It was closely written between the lines, and she couldn't begin to guess what the invisible writing said.

But the drive to Sigtuna was interesting, and the little lakeside village charming with narrow streets and rows of small shops, golden birches reflected like yellow fires in the lake, and children from a nearby school shouting.

The Backes' house was painted dark red in the conventional Swedish style. Willa had written in her diary that she would paint her cottage pink, what the Swedes needed was a little frivolity. Frivolity was the last word that could be used about the Backes' house, or the Backe family itself. Everything was exactly as Willa had described it, Mama Backe sitting in an armchair with her plump white hands folded neatly one over the other in her lap, her black dress pinned across her large bosom with an enormous cameo brooch, her grey hair dragged into an uncompromising knot on the top of her head, her little mouth pursed into wrinkles, her eyes glinting behind steel-rimmed spectacles. Papa Backe tall, thin, cadaverous, his complete lack of interest in the visitors suggesting a slight senility. The formidable Ulrika bustling about with plates of food, and cups of tea, the latter made especially for the English guest. And Doctor Sven Backe who seemed only to acquire authority and masculinity when he was in his surgery. Certainly he had little when under the watchful eyes of his mother and sister.

He would do better if he ran off with his eager nurse, Grace thought. Anything would be better than this smothering atmosphere.

But the setting of the house was attractive.

Through the lace curtains Grace could see the feathery rushes bending over the lake in the bitter wind. Golden leaves whirled, too light and papery to settle.

"It's really pretty here in the summer," Sven said. "Crowded, of course. Everyone comes to swim or sail."

"We like it best in the winter," Ulrika, with her winter face, was saying nothing unexpected. "It's quiet and private then. It belongs to the permanent residents. The snow falls and the lake is frozen over, and we have large fires. Isn't it nicest then, Sven?"

"It's a good time for working," Sven agreed.

"My brother is writing a thesis," Ulrika told Grace with pride. "He likes to have his time uninterrupted."

It seemed that Mama Backe didn't speak English, although her watchful eyes suggested she understood more than she admitted. She occasionally made a remark to Ulrika or Sven in Swedish. The old man at the other side of the fire was entirely silent.

Willa in this household was utterly incongruous. Whatever had they made of her when she had visited?

Yet she must have been of importance, for Ebba was making a point of telling Sven and Ulrika about the letter from her.

"Grace was so relieved to get it. Weren't you, Grace? I believe you thought she had been abducted."

Ulrika gave a single exclamation of laughter.

"Who by, I wonder? Not Sven!"

"Don't be ridiculous, Ulrika," Sven said crossly.

"Well, you have to admit there was a rumour at the beginning that you had been engaged to marry her."

"There were rumours about everyone she had ever been seen with. You know that as well as I do. After all, she was only here once, for a weekend, and with several other people." The dark melancholy eyes rested on Grace. "We went swimming, and sailing. The Sinclairs were here, too. And Bill Jordan."

"If there were to be rumours about anyone, it should have been about Bill Jordan," Ulrika said decisively. "Still, he didn't live long enough to tell the tale."

Grace looked at Sven. "It must have been terrible for you having to give evidence about a friend's death."

"That's all in the life of a doctor," Sven answered. "It was quite obviously an accident. I never had any doubt about that."

"And why," said Ebba lazily, "must we get on to this unhappy subject again? Or on to that silly cousin of yours, Grace, for that matter. I've told you I'm really so enormously bored with her."

"So are we all," said Ulrika, putting the teapot down with a thud. She added something in Swedish to her mother, and the old lady nodded several times, her sharp eyes on Grace. Were they discussing whether she might have designs on Sven? Were they suspicious of every single woman who came within his orbit? Well, whatever the initial rumours had been about him and Willa, one could entirely discount them now. They were too incongruous. Willa would have run miles from this depressing household.

Grace said as much to Ebba on the way home, and Ebba gave her low satirical laugh.

"Good heavens, Grace, did you think Willa and Sven might have had a thing. Impossible. He'll never escape his mother, much less that dreadful sister. Not that he wouldn't like to."

"Would he?"

"Well, again, perhaps not. People can get attached to their prisons."

"Is his thesis important?"

"I believe so. He's very clever. He wants to be famous. Ulrika wants him to be, too, but when the time comes she'll change her mind. It might take him away from her. People are too complicated. They make such problems for themselves. I'm sorry for Sven, having that family round his neck, but I also want to shake him for not pushing them off."

Grace was moderately certain that Willa would have had the same reactions. A man like Sven could not have been of any more than momentary interest to her. Yet he was a significant part of her diary. Sven, Axel, Jacob, Gustav . . .

But Gustav didn't exist, except in another guise. Or did he?

For a curious overheard remark gave Grace a wakeful night. The attics creaked, to be sure, but Ebba's low words to Jacob, by the fire in the library after Grace had said good night and then returned to ask for a book to read, were more disturbing. "Gustav will arrange it, of course. Who else?"

Ebba had jumped at Grace's appearance, her pallid face staring out of the gloom of a dying fire and burnt-down candles.

"You came in so quietly. Is there something the matter?"

"I just wanted to beg a book to read, if you have any in English."

"Masses. Help yourself." Ebba yawned. "I must go to bed. Are you coming, Jacob? Put your accounts away. The worries of running an estate with not enough staff, Grace. No one should envy us."

So Gustav was an employee. Why not? It was a common name in Sweden. Or was Ebba's oblique explanation a little too deliberate?

THE SINCLAIR children hurtled up the steps to the front door. Their parents' ascent was more leisurely, Kate's slow, Peter's positively a crawl.

"Poor Peter has had the bug now," Kate explained. "Haven't you, darling. He isn't infectious but he's still frail."

Peter, his eyes dull and dark-circled, his skin yellowish, did look frail and lethargic.

"The trouble was he wouldn't go to bed," Kate went on. "And he's working awfully late at nights."

"Had to," said Peter. "Do shut up, Kate. Rushed jobs are rushed jobs. Anyway, I never could stick staying in bed with a thermometer. Are we getting some shooting today?"

"If you feel up to it," Jacob said, and Ebba, greeting both Kate and Peter with light kisses, added, "We're having an early lunch, and then you men can do what you please. Sven and Ulrika are here."

It was a grey day with a low dark sky. For cosiness, Ebba had drawn the curtains in the dining room and lit candles, purple, red and green ones in the sconces round the walls. Their light was reflected in the glass on the table, bowls and tumblers of Orrefors and

Kosta, so heavy that you could drop one on someone's toes and break them, Grace reflected. Or on someone's head. But no one here was going to be throwing brandy glasses about. They were all such good friends, and they enjoyed their formalities so much. All the "skolling" that must go on, to the hostess, to each guest separately. Even Ulrika managed to present a pleasant countenance and proved to be quite jolly with the Sinclair children. She had them eating their food with obedient dispatch on the promise that later she would take them up to the attics to play their favourite game of dressing up.

"You don't mind, do you, Ebba?" she asked.

"Not in the least. I keep old theatrical costumes up there," Ebba explained to Grace. "And there are boxes of bits and pieces from Jacob's family. Some old military uniforms. Alexander likes wearing a sword, don't you, darling?"

Alexander wriggled with pleasure. Georgy said that she wanted the hat with the ostrich feathers. She would so dearly like it to be her own, to take home.

"Georgy!" Kate admonished.

"Why not?" said Ebba lazily. "Can you see me ever wearing it?"

"She mustn't ask for things."

"Being a woman she must test her persuasive powers," Ebba said. "Don't you men agree?"

The men laughed, but Kate had her head down, the familiar frown between her eyes. She didn't like Ebba, Grace realised. She probably hated coming here. But there seemed to be so little she did like, one began to feel sorrier for Peter all the time. He had scarcely touched his food, but he had had his wine glass filled more than once, and was beginning to look better. By the end of the meal he had got back his attractive animation and the yellow tinge had left his face. He was impatient to get outdoors before the early twilight came down.

"We should have two hours of daylight. Let's make the most of it."

"Peter!" Kate's eyes were on Peter's empty glass. "Should you? I mean—"

"Are you suggesting I can't shoot straight after three glasses of wine?"

"I was only thinking—" Kate stopped, and Grace knew that she had been going to mention Bill Jordan.

"For God's sake, stop fussing!" Peter exclaimed.

"I was only going to say you may still have a temperature. I don't want to nurse you through pneumonia."

"I'll take care of him, Kate," said Sven in what was obviously his best bedside manner. "If it's too cold we'll come home."

"How far are we from your cottage?" Grace asked Kate idly. "I've got completely mixed up. There's always an arm of the lake, wherever we go."

"Oh, it's about ten miles away. Isn't it, Peter?"

"Something like that," Peter said. "We've locked it up for the winter. It'll be snowed up before long."

"Until the beginning of May," Kate sighed. "All those dark months."

It was cosy by the fire in the big dark hall. Grace half dozed, and Ebba went unashamedly to sleep, her elegant head tipped sideways against the cushions of her chair. Kate had knitting, a half-finished child's sweater, but she kept stopping work, as if she were too deep in thought to concentrate. From the attics the sound of the children's voices, occasionally accompanied by Ulrika's unexpected laughter, came faintly. Ulrika was explained, now. She had too much maternal instinct, and no one but her elderly parents and her brother to expend it on. Everyone, Grace thought sleepily, became harmless when their idiosyncrasies were interpreted.

The peace of the afternoon was shattered, however, when the children erupted into the room to show their costumes.

"Look at me!" shrieked Georgy. "I'm a lady."

She was tottering on high heels, and had the coveted ostrich-plumed hat tipped crookedly over one eye. One hand held up a long satin skirt, the other clutched at a skinny leopard-skin fur tippet tied round her neck.

Alexander, in an ancient military jacket that reached to his ankles, marched about noisily, trailing a sheathed sword.

"Alexander is supposed to be my boy friend," Georgy said, doubling up with giggles.

"I'm going to fight a war," Alexander announced. "I'm going to slash off people's heads."

"Georgy," said Kate in a curiously still voice, "where did you get that piece of fur?"

204

"Out of the box. Why, Mummy?"

"I just thought—I had seen it before."

Ebba, who had been looking at the children in tolerant amusement, looked again at Georgy. Something flickered in her eyes, momentarily. Then she was laughing lazily.

"One of Jacob's aunts had a passion for bits of fur. There's a box full of moth-eaten pieces. She must have looked like an old cat."

Georgy burst into shrieks of laughter.

"Do I look like an old cat, Mummy?"

"It's like a tie Willa had," said Kate in the same still voice.

"Not that woman again!" exclaimed Ulrika, bustling in. "How would her fur piece be here?"

"Yes, how would it?" Ebba asked. "Unless she left it here and one of the maids put it in the dressing-up box by mistake."

"She dropped things around," Kate murmured, staring at Grace. "Her sun-glasses by the lake, for instance."

Ulrika examined the piece of spotted fur round Georgy's neck.

"It's only—what do you call it?—simulated. If it's Willa's I suppose she hardly thought it worth looking for."

"Then it serves her right to lose it," Ebba

205

said. "Anyone who has the bad taste to wear fake fur—why are you looking like that, Grace?"

How was she looking? Deeply startled because she had suddenly remembered Fru Lindstrom's description of Willa's clothes when she had left on her hopeful elopement? "Her spotted fur hat and a piece round her neck to match . . ."

So that this had been lost *after* her disappearance from Stockholm. And now it had turned up in an attic at the von Sturpes. If, of course, it were the same piece . . .

Grace managed to speak normally.

"I suppose I'm surprised because my landlady said Willa was wearing leopard skin when she eloped."

"But real, surely, for a wedding," Ebba insisted. "Even Willa couldn't wear that ratty old bit to be married in. Could she?"

She sounded so plausible. Everyone always sounded plausible when Willa was discussed. Nevertheless, with all her fakes, her sunglasses, her false eyelashes, her dyed hair, Willa would be uncritically happy in her faked furs. She would regard it as a foolish waste of money to buy real ones.

Therefore, although Ebba obviously had no

intention of admitting it, Willa must have been here very recently.

Grace put out her hand to Georgy.

"If that's Willa's I'll have it, please."

"But, Grace—" Ebba didn't care for that too much. Then she gave her breathy laugh. "Take it if you want to. I hope the ghost of Jacob's aunt won't come claiming it."

"I don't think so. Willa can collect it when she collects the rest of her stuff. But I do think it awfully strange that it should be here."

For a moment no one spoke. Then Kate sat up, saying in distaste, "Georgy! Alexander! Go and take those awful old clothes off. I'm sorry Ebba. But clothes after people have—I just mean, they give me the creeps."

THE MEN CAME back just after dark. They were mud-splashed, and looked tired, especially Peter whose face had gone that unhealthy yellowish colour again.

"No luck," said Jacob.

"None?" It seemed as if Ebba were disappointed. Her strange eyes flickered again. Did she enjoy seeing the blood-stained carcass of an elk dragged home?

"We only found tracks," said Sven. He

threw himself into a chair wearily, ignoring his muddy state. But Peter walked about restlessly, saying that they must get on the way. Where were the children? Couldn't Kate rustle them up quickly?

Grace made an abrupt decision.

"Ebba, would you mind if I took the opportunity of a lift with Peter and Kate, and went back this evening instead of in the morning?"

She didn't care about rudeness. She suddenly didn't trust Ebba, and wanted overpoweringly to get back to tell Polsen everything that had happened.

Ebba's manners, it seemed, were equal to the sudden ungracious departure of guests. Or could it be that she was relieved?

"Why, of course, Grace. Though we've loved your visit and it seems awfully short." Before she could say more, the telephone rang, and she stretched out her hand for it. "Jacob, get everyone a drink. Hallo! Who is that?"

She was an accomplished actress. After all, she had admitted that acting had been her profession. But even her poise was slightly shaken by whoever her caller was. Grace saw her hand tighten round the receiver. Her long narrow face was set.

"What! You didn't—but that's impossible! No, I can't talk now. I have guests. The men have just come in from shooting. Call me later and tell me in detail."

She put down the receiver with a bang and swore softly to herself, then apologised, giving her small laugh.

"Now if that isn't the limit. Jacob, that work I'd arranged—no, never mind. I mustn't bore everyone with domestic problems. Where's my drink? Didn't you get me one?"

Gustav, who was to have arranged that mysterious work, had let her down, Grace was thinking bemusedly. It must have been a very important task, for her to lose her composure. What was more, her uneasiness had communicated itself to everyone else, and for a moment the room was quiet.

Then Peter said loudly, "Bad show. But that's how it is nowadays, isn't it? You can't delegate. Kate, haven't you called the kids? We've got to be off. Sure, we'll give you a lift, Grace, but you'll have to be ready in ten minutes."

HE DROVE much too fast all the way to Stockholm. Kate was nervous, sitting tensely beside him, sometimes turning her head to look at him. In the back Grace, with an arm round each child, was exhilarated by the speed, and only glad to be getting home quickly. Perhaps there would be some more news from Willa. At least Polsen would be there.

"I gather Ebba doesn't like being thwarted," she said, at one stage. "She seemed upset about that thing she wanted done."

"I'm sure I wouldn't like to defy her," Kate said. "She terrifies me. How did you enjoy your weekend, Grace?"

"It was interesting."

"You're being diplomatic."

"I liked Sigtuna. It was pretty."

"Ghastly place," said Peter.

Kate looked at him in surprise.

"But I thought you liked it. You always wanted to go there in the summer."

"Well, now it's winter, and I don't want to go anywhere. We're staying home for the duration."

Kate shrugged. "Goodness, you are touchy. I believe you've got a temperature again. I told you we shouldn't have gone out today."

More to change the subject than anything,

Grace said, "Wasn't it strange about finding Willa's fur? I'm inclined to agree with Ebba. It is a rather horrid article."

"Willa's fur?" said Peter. "Where?"

"It had got in the dressing-up boxes in the attics," Kate answered. "Willa must have left it lying around like she did other belongings."

Peter was reflecting. "That night she got tight on schnapps," he exclaimed. "Don't you remember? We had to take her home."

"Was she wearing her fur that day? Wasn't it in the summer?"

"Late summer. Chilly. We all got a bit merry that day. I wouldn't have dared drive the car if I hadn't got diplomatic immunity."

"But what I don't understand," Grace said deliberately, "is how Fru Lindstrom could have thought Willa was wearing that fur piece the day she eloped."

"Is that what the nosey old girl said?" Peter spoke without apparent interest, though after a pause. "She could have been mistaken. Witnesses often are. They have preconceived pictures in their minds. Oh, what the hell!"

"I know," said Grace. "Willa, with or without her tatty fur piece, is getting to be a bore."

"You've said it, love. And how!"

THERE WAS silence again for several miles. The forest and the empty fields receded and the city lights grew bright. Alexander snuggled against Grace, half asleep.

"I'm glad there was no elks," he murmured.

"*Were* no elks," Georgy corrected. "You still talk like a baby."

"Isn't no elks today," Alexander said contentedly.

11

"**B**ACK already, Froken Asherton! I hope you had a better time than poor Captain Morgensson. He is in a fine state, I can tell you. Some of his cargo has been delayed and he wanted to sail tomorrow. Now he has wharfage troubles, and goodness knows what." Fru Lindstrom's hands were in their familiar upflung position. She was studying Grace's demeanour for signs of more drama, for which she was obviously an addict.

"I'm sorry for Captain Morgensson," Grace said perfunctorily, though what did she care for that cold staring man? "Yes, I had a nice time, thank you. Is everything all right?"

Fru Lindstrom clapped her hands together, suddenly remembering another gleeful secret.

"Everything is fine, Froken Asherton. But judge for yourself when you go upstairs."

Since one never knew whether Fru Lindstrom's glee came from pleasure at another person's good fortune or misfortune, Grace went upstairs in some apprehension. Willa? she was thinking inevitably.

As soon as she opened the door she knew someone had been in the flat. What was different? Nothing, it seemed. Everything was orderly, as she had left it, the cushions straight, the bed undisturbed.

But no! There was a cover over the birdcage in the corner, and under it, sleepy on his perch, a fine yellow canary.

Grace dropped the cover and flew up the stairs to Polsen's door. If he weren't in—he *had* to be in!

The door opened and he stood there, large, solid, tentative, his thick eyebrows raised over his mild eyes.

"Oh, Polsen, how darling! The canary!"

He gave his slow pleased smile. "You knew it was me?"

"Of *course*! Who else would think of something so nice?"

Polsen stood aside to let her go in.

"We weren't expecting you until the morning. The bird was to be singing in welcome."

"We?"

"Magnus and myself. Magnus chose the bird. He said this one was the best specimen."

"How adorable! I always hated that empty cage. Of course how I smuggle a canary into England is another thing. It is mine to take to England, isn't it?"

"If you insist on returning."

"Of course I'll have to go home. Don't be silly. Polsen! Isn't that Willa's diary?"

"The canary moved into the cage, and the diary moved out." He stopped being facetious and added, "I've been going through it again. With a fine tooth comb, I believe the expression is."

"Have you any new ideas? Has something happened this weekend?"

"You tell me. No, first I'll tell you that I have found the king with two queens."

"Where?"

"In Uppsala cathedral. King Gustav Vasa with his great beard lying between his two beautiful little queens."

More symbolism!

"What significance has that got?" Grace asked disappointedly.

"A belated significance, I'm afraid. I think Willa was telling us that her Gustav was already married. She was to be his second wife."

"We know that."

"Now. We didn't when we first read the diary, when we were meant to pick up these clues."

"And according to you both of the wives dead!" Grace protested.

"That's interpreting too broadly, I think. Come and sit down and tell me about your weekend. Did Ebba give you a gay time?"

"I hardly think gay is the right word. I want to know first what you were doing in Uppsala."

"Just wandering about. Drinking too much coffee in cafés. Asking about rooms to let, or even summer cottages that weren't shut up for the winter. Whether foreign visitors stayed on after the snow began."

"And did you get any interesting answers?" Grace asked tensely.

"No. Not one. I only found the king and his queens. Which doesn't mean that we now begin to look for someone with a long beard. Tell me what happened to you."

Grace sat on the floor in front of the fat-bellied stove, her head against Polsen's knees, and felt her tension ebbing away as the events of the weekend were told.

"They all know something," she finished. "All of them. Why won't they tell me what it is? Why am I supposed to be shown how normal and innocent everything is? That horrid bit of fur wasn't meant to turn up, of course. I'm like Kate. It gives me the creeps. I get this feeling that something much worse than an old bit of fake fur will turn up."

When Polsen didn't speak, she went on, "Ebba insisted that Willa would have had the real thing for her wedding outfit. Do you know if she went shopping for leopard skin?"

"No, I don't, but my guess is that if she were in the market for real fur it would have been mink."

"So," said Grace slowly.

"So."

The fire glowed inside the stove. Grace tried to think only of the comfort and warmth in this room.

"Did the canary sing to you?" she asked.

"Like an opera star."

"Then it will to me, in the morning." Her smile died. "Polsen, what am I to do next?"

"Wait."

"For Willa? But I've done nothing else—"

"We'll both go to Uppsala next Saturday. Or perhaps Wednesday if I can arrange for Oscar Johannson to take my class."

"Even that's two days away," Grace said impatiently.

"If all those people know something, as you say, it can't be so bad. Do you understand?"

"There's safety in numbers? But if only one person knew it would be a deadly secret?"

"That's what I mean," said Polsen in his imperturbable way.

IN THE NIGHT a gale blew up. Great luminous clouds floated over the moon, and tendrils of cold air somehow crept through the closed windows and made the room chilly. The dawn sky was a beautiful pearled pink, radiant and pure. A pink heaven for the sorrowful Swedes, Grace thought, getting out of bed and leaning on the windowsill. The wind was still buffeting at the window, and the streets below were alive with crazily whirling golden leaves. The boats rocked at anchor. The dark whipped-up water of the harbour looked chillingly cold.

But presently the pink faded out of the sky, the sun came up, and as the room lightened, the canary, hopefully uncovered by Grace, began to sing.

Her eyes filled with tears of pleasure. Dear

Polsen! Did he know she always associated Willa, with her yellow hair, with that empty cage? Willa, the canary that flew away. But now here was a vigorously alive little occupant, so one had to believe that Willa was vigorously alive, too. Well, alive, anyway.

Polsen had gone downstairs some time ago. Now Grace heard Captain Morgensson leaving, calling *"Farval"* to his aunts in his loud voice, and banging every door behind him. She watched from the window and presently saw him cross the street, his knapsack over his shoulder, his nautical cap tipped over one eye. He walked with a long swinging stride, purposefully. Grace wondered if he were intending to sail without the cargo that had failed to be loaded.

Because she had nothing else to do that day (Wait, Polsen had said, and the prospect was unbearably tedious), she decided to pay a call on the Misses Morgensson.

She was greeted with cries of pleasure.

"But do come in, my dear," exclaimed Miss Anna. "We are always lonely when Axel has gone."

"Is he sailing today?"

"*Ja.* He was so angry yesterday, there was a delay about some important cargo. At first he thought he would have to wait for it, but this morning he said if it didn't arrive before midday he would sail without it, important or not. He was very annoyed, being a person for strict discipline."

So exit Axel, it seemed. Which left gentle Jacob, gloomy Sven. And Gustav?

"Did you hear my canary singing this morning?" Grace asked.

"You have a canary! But how charming."

"Herre Polsen got it for me."

"Ah ha!" Miss Anna wagged a coy finger. "I think Herre Polsen is getting fond of you, Froken Asherton. He is a lonely man. You won't leave us too soon, I hope, like Froken Bedford?"

"She is back?" said Miss Katerina, cupping her hand to her ear.

"*Nej*, Katerina. I didn't say she was back. I only hoped Froken Asherton wouldn't leave us too suddenly."

A sudden flurry of yellow leaves blew against the window. It would be stormy for Axel to go to sea. But it was cosy in here, the bright room, the two old papery faces with their friendly eyes and shawled shoulders, the pot plants, the smell of hot coffee, the absence of Axel with his hard stare.

220

Grace was reluctant to leave. In spite of the cheering presence of the canary Willa's flat was still too empty. Things happened in there. Such as the telephone ringing the moment she unlocked the door. She had the feeling that it had been ringing like that, urgently, all the time she had been out.

"Grace! Peter told me to tell you—the police will be calling—oh, it's too awful—"

Kate's voice was almost incoherent. Distinctly Grace felt a shiver travel down her spine, spread over her whole body.

"Willa?" she whispered with shocked inevitability.

"Yes, Willa. She's been found."

"Found! Where? Why doesn't she ring me herself? Hasn't anyone told her I'm here?"

Grace checked herself. She was beginning to gabble like Kate, putting off the moment when she must listen to what Kate had to tell her.

"She can't ring you herself. Because she's dead!" Kate's voice was rising in hysteria. "Some schoolchildren found her in the lake at Sigtuna. Among all those rushes. You know, where we used to swim."

Yesterday, no, Saturday, she had looked at the very place. She had admired the graceful feathery rushes reflected in the water, not knowing what lay beneath their reflection. Willa, with her drowned face, her streaming yellow hair.

"Grace, are you there? Are you all right?"

"Is that where she—fell in?" Grace had closed her eyes to try to shut out the scene. But this was a mistake, for it made it more clear than ever, the horrified schoolchildren, the bitter wind over the disturbed grey water, the fallen birch leaves trampled into the mud.

"They don't know. They think—the body might have floated a distance until the storm last night washed it up." There was a sharply indrawn breath at the other end of the telephone and Kate gasped, "I have to go. I feel sick."

"You don't! You have to tell me more."

"That's all," Kate wailed. "Willa's dead."

"Who told you and Peter?"

"The police rang the Embassy. Peter says the Ambassador is in a state. It's so awful, after Bill Jordan. Peter's had to be questioned for hours, because she was his secretary. But that's all I *know*!"

"You must know more. What do the police think?"

"Suicide, of course. She was pregnant and

the man's let her down. This Gustav has let her down. Grace, I can hear the children coming in. I really have to go."

The telephone clicked, and Grace sat down, slowly and carefully, as if she had grown old and brittle-boned.

Willa dead. No, it wasn't true. Not silly, noisy, impulsive, gregarious Willa, trusting everyone, ready for anything. Maybe Wilhelmina, with her silent cry of desperation, could die. Because she had loved her mysterious Gustav, and he had failed her, and she couldn't face having his child alone. The Swedes wouldn't find the suicide of a young woman in that condition too surprising. Pathetic, unfortunate and unnecessary, but not suspicious.

Whereas Willa, with her canary hair, her gaiety, was quite incapable of taking her own life. Grace knew that. She wondered if she would be able to convince the police of this fact when they came.

She was still sitting in the same position, rigid, in a state of shock, when the telephone rang again.

"Grace," said Peter Sinclair in a quiet dull voice Grace hardly recognised, "has Kate told you?"

"Yes, but I don't believe it."

"You'll have to, I'm afraid. I just wanted to warn you, the police will be asking you to go to Uppsala to identify the body."

"Uppsala," she said stupidly. Where Polsen had been on Saturday, looking at the dead queens in the cathedral. Now the very name had a sinister sound.

"That's where they've taken her. I'm sorry, do you think you can face it?"

"If I have to."

"Good girl. You're a bloody marvel. You sound so calm. Do you want me to come with you?"

"No, thank you." Of course she sounded calm. How could she speak with animation when she was filled with ice? "If anyone comes it must be Polsen."

"Polsen!" She thought Peter sounded affronted. What did that matter? No one but Polsen had listened to her foreboding about Willa, no one else had cared. So why should Peter begin to care now, except for the very important reason that there was another scandal to be hushed up?

"Are you sure, Grace?"

"That he'll come? Of course he will."

"Well, then—I admit I don't relish such a

grisly task. By the way, if you see the children, Kate and I want it kept from them. And what are you going to tell the police?"

"Everything, of course."

"Not all this tarrydiddle about Willa's belongings dropped around, and the kids saying she was on the telephone the other day, and the chap with a key getting into your flat."

"Chap?" How old-fashioned Peter was sounding with his 'tarrydiddle'.

"Well, of course he was a chap. When did Willa have girl friends?" Peter's voice was rough with tension. "Be a bit circumspect, Grace, or the ambassador won't like it."

"It's a pity about the ambassador!"

"We don't want to be another Bonn."

"Your precious reputation!" Grace burst out. "Is that all you're thinking of?"

"And Willa's. Which could do with a bit of a whitewash, if you must know."

Grace hadn't thought Peter could be so callous. Perhaps that was a characteristic that came out in all good diplomats when the side was threatened. Form a square, fall back on your ranks, never mind sacrificing the unimportant innocent for the bigger cause.

For Willa was an innocent, whatever everybody said.

And now she was dead. One had to keep probing at that hard cold stone of knowledge in one's heart. And come to the inevitable decision.

"If *you* must know, Peter," she said, "I don't for one minute believe this is suicide. So I still intend to give the police all the evidence I have, including Willa's diary."

She had startled him then. She heard his indrawn breath.

"You never told me anything about finding a diary."

"No. That was in the days when I was being discreet," Grace said, without humour.

"What's in it? Anything significant?"

"I think so. Tell the ambassador."

She hung up. She was suddenly deadly tired. She could visualise Peter's indignant face, his eyes slightly protruding, his mouth hard as she had seen it when he was angry with his wife. His merry-boy charm had another personality behind it. Naturally. He wouldn't be in his present job without the ability to present a completely unemotional front when necessary.

But at this minute Grace couldn't forgive

him for not being on Willa's side. Let him sweat over what he must now be imagining were her scandalous secrets in the diary.

For Willa was dead, and she, Grace, had to go and look at what was now called simply 'the body' and write to her father and arrange about a funeral and get rid of that wardrobe full of clothes.

Did any of those stiff-upper-lipped people at the Embassy give a thought to the agony of these things?

12

THE two policemen, the officer and the sergeant, sat in the front of the car, Polsen and herself in the back. The police had been more than willing for Polsen to come. They spoke English but without a wide vocabulary. Herre Polsen would be useful as an interpreter. There were a great many questions to be asked even if, as seemed likely, the cause of death was suicide by drowning. And it was easy enough to drown in this cold weather. One had only to fall in the lake accidentally and one would be frozen to death within minutes.

Polsen asked, in a pedantic schoolmasterish way, how long the body had been immersed and was told that it was probably one or two days. It was not thought that the death fall, or whatever it had been, had taken place at Sigtuna. It was too populated a spot, with schoolchildren or fishermen or visitors from the city always wandering about at the lake's edge. The body must have floated a distance in the storm. There was the possibility it had fallen overboard from a boat. But that supposition was untenable unless one were to begin thinking in terms of murder, which was scarcely in anyone's mind. The young lady was four to five months pregnant. If every man murdered the girl he got in the family way there wouldn't be enough police or enough prisons in the country.

The two policemen, with their cropped fair heads and thick pink necks, both laughed jovially. Drowning wasn't so bad, one of them said. Better than the mutilated death a great many people met in car smashes.

Polsen sat hunched in his corner of the seat, making no attempt to touch Grace reassuringly, or even to smile at her. He had been like that ever since they had picked him up at the university. He was deeply shocked by the news, but somehow not surprised. Definitely not surprised. Now there was no reading the expression in his blank eyes, his withdrawn face.

He hadn't expected to be in Uppsala again so soon, Grace thought. Or had he?

They couldn't talk while those two guardians of the law sat in the front seat. Grace said that Fru Lindstrom was looking after the canary. Cage birds liked company, and even Fru

Lindstrom temporarily shocked into speechlessness by the tragedy, would be better than nobody. The Misses Morgensson had not been told. Why distress such old ladies? And their nephew Axel's ship had sailed at noon. For some reason the police had taken the trouble to establish that fact.

The reaction of the von Sturpes, the Backes, Winifred Wright and others, would come later. In the meantime a thin green church spire on the skyline indicated that Uppsala was near. There were crows swinging low in the sky, squawking, and along the banks of the canal, hatted and overcoated Swedes, solemnly strolling. A bitter wind blew down the narrow streets. Opposite the cathedral and the university buildings there was the inevitable cemetery, the motionless dark tall trees and the frozen gravestones.

And in a square hygienic ugly room, Willa, frozen too, finally silent.

There was a chance to talk to Polsen after all. Grace was aware that she must have looked almost as ghastly as what she had had to gaze on, in that horrible silent little room, for one of the police suggested that Polsen take her for some coffee at a café down the street. The sergeant could drop them there and pick them up in half an hour or so. It was an ordeal doing this sort of thing for the first time. Or for any number of times, if it came to that. One never quite got used to it, especially when the victim was young.

At first Grace thought the coffee would make her sick. She held the warm liquid in her mouth, and determined to swallow it, but slowly. She couldn't be sick in front of Polsen, in this nice clean café with its view of the canal. It must be a charming view in summer when the slow-flowing water sparkled and the overhanging trees were green. The houses along the opposite bank were old and dignified, with long flights of steps and interesting doorways. The scene would have been Parisian if there had been more colour and sunshine. But the sluggish black water reflected the grey sky. The floating yellow leaves, dropped from the overhanging birches, heightened the melancholy.

Looking at the water made Grace think of that dreadful swollen sodden face and the hair from which all the canary colour had been washed. She took another valiant swallow of coffee and said, "It's all right, Polsen. I'm not going to disgrace you."

"How could you do that?"

At last he touched her hand, taking it in his and holding it in his lap. She shivered violently.

"I'm frozen. That lake water must have been icy. Polsen, she wouldn't have killed herself. Because that would have killed the baby, and it was the baby she was holding out for. Otherwise she'd have had an abortion when it was offered, wouldn't she?"

"Was it offered?"

"It must have been. It would have saved Gustav getting that divorce that I'm sure he didn't want. Wouldn't it?"

"You keep asking me. I don't know."

"You know well enough. Gustav is a rat and we've got to find him. I've given the police Willa's diary."

"So I hear."

The briefness of Polsen's answer made her say, "Do you object, too?"

"Why should I? Who does?"

"The Embassy. At least Peter Sinclair felt he had to, as its spokesman. Well, they might have been able to claim diplomatic immunity with Bill Jordan, but they can't with Willa since she was no longer a member of the staff. So they'll just have to make the best of the publicity."

"It won't be more than a day's sensation," Polsen said. "Not even that. A girl taking her life because she's pregnant and unhappy and deserted. It happens all the time."

"But that isn't how it happened this time. Gustav will tell us. When we find him."

"That's up to the police now, isn't it? After all, it isn't a crime to make a girl pregnant."

"No, but it is to drown her," Grace said so vehemently that the woman behind the counter stared at them, blinking her pale lashes.

"You're jumping to conclusions, Grace. Your mind is more logical than this. Have another cup of coffee. We have time."

"I'm not myself any more," Grace muttered. "I've begun to think like Willa. Ever since I wore her clothes and put on her scent. I've got illogical and liable to act on hunches. Impulsive. Irrational, perhaps. Perhaps not. Perhaps I'm really myself without knowing it." She rubbed her eyes wearily. "I might end up in Lake Malaren, too, mightn't I?"

"Grace, don't be crazy! You must go back to England."

"Before the winter madness gets me? Like it's getting Kate Sinclair. Peter, too, a bit, I think. And it must have got Willa some time ago. All that gothic stuff she wrote in her diary."

"Willa had an undisciplined imagination, and you have a disciplined one." Whatever storm was going on in Grace's head, Polsen was keeping his customary quiet honest good sense. "For instance, instead of talking about a king with two queens in that roundabout way, wouldn't you have said simply that Gustav has two wives, and one has to be got rid of before the other one can be happy?"

Grace looked at him, her eyes wide.

"But, Polsen, that's it! Now I realise! Willa was the wife to be got rid of, not the one to be saved!"

The police said it was unfortunate that no one seemed to know where Willa had been living just prior to her death. They were inclined to dismiss the diary, all that nonsense about 'the rain on the roof and the dark forest' as fanciful. And as to the unidentified Gustav looking like a portrait in Gripsholm Castle, a great many Swedes had similar characteristics, blue eyes, blond hair, thick lips. Nevertheless, they would make a search. The dead girl's possessions must be somewhere. Her handbag, for instance. Did Grace and Polsen know that a woman seldom jumped in a lake with her handbag. Some careful instinct, preserved even at that desperate moment, made her leave it safely on the bank.

But they had not yet ascertained where the tragedy had happened. The investigation might take some time. The lake was very large.

The only items of any value that Willa had been wearing were a gold wrist watch and a ring. The ring was lapis lazuli with an intricate antique gold setting. Did Grace know anything about it?

"Only what the girls at the Embassy told me," Grace answered. "They said that Gustav—the man she ran off with—had given it to her. I don't know whether he had bought it in Stockholm. It might have been in his family. It was old, the girls said."

"*Ja*," said the men. That was all.

IN WILLA'S FLAT nothing had visibly altered. Only the sense of waiting and expectation was gone. Grace said goodnight to Polsen on the doorstep. She had to put a telephone call through to her father, an ordeal she dreaded almost as much as the trip to Uppsala. She also, sooner or later, had to go through

Willa's things, make a decision about the funeral, write to Willa's friends.

The nightmare evening turned into a real nightmare when Grace tried to sleep. She tossed and turned and then, in a light sleep, dreamed that Willa was trying to push her out of the pretty Gustav III bed, saying that that was her bed, she wanted to come back.

Her skin prickling with horror, Grace leapt out of bed and out of the flat, running up the stairs in her nightgown. She rattled at Polsen's door, found it unlocked and burst into the dark room, groping her way to Polsen's bed.

"Let me come in," she whispered. "I'm scared. I hate being alone."

The bedclothes were thrown back and his arm pulled her in beside him. He held her face against his breast, his chin pressing into her hair.

"I wasn't asleep, either," he said in a warm grumble.

"It's enough that Willa's alone tonight. Not us."

"I agree. Not us."

Gradually Grace stopped shivering. She realised that Polsen slept naked. The skin of his chest was smooth and hairless. His heart

236

beat with a slow steady thud beneath her cheekbone. She liked feeling that, it was so strong and reassuring, it would go on forever.

Presently he said, "Haven't you too many clothes on?"

Silently she sat up and pulled her nightgown over her head, then slid down into the narrow bed, her heart beating against his.

"Grace?"

"Yes, Polsen. Please!"

Deftly and tenderly his big body covered hers. And it was right, because the nightmare stopped. The blood was singing in her veins, she was alive, alive, alive. And somewhere Willa was laughing.

"Fancy you, Grace."

She laughed herself, although the sound was more like a sob, and fell asleep, wrapped in Polsen's arms.

When she awoke the arms had gone. She was alone in the bed, but there was a pleasant smell of coffee, and Polsen was saying, "Breakfast is ready. How do you like your coffee?"

"With milk, please."

He handed her her nightgown.

"Not that I don't like you like that, but it's

a cold morning. Today I believe it really will snow."

"Polsen—"

He had his back to her as he stood at the table, pouring coffee.

"Yes? But if you're going to talk about last night, this isn't the time."

She nodded. He was right, as he usually was. He knew she was the kind to explain, to interpret, even to apologise. She might even begin to think that the reason for her behaviour was that Willa had been getting inside her again, and that would be disastrous.

"Polsen, I think I love you," she said.

That seemed safe enough, for he looked pleased.

"You only think? That's my sober Grace."

Not Willa. Thank Heaven. He hadn't been thinking it a Willa thing last night.

"Well, do you love me? Polsen?"

"I told you this isn't the time to have this kind of conversation. There are too many things involved. But if you're asking, was I happy last night, I was. Now don't let your coffee get cold. By the way, I've arranged not to go back to the university this week, so anything I can do, I will be available."

But what was there to do except answer the telephone? Grace listened to her father's voice, incongruously from a peaceful Suffolk village.

"Grace, I simply didn't take in what you told me last night. Is this terrible thing about Willa true?"

"I saw her, Daddy, I told you."

"Good God! It's unbelievable. Do you want me to fly over?"

"No, no, you mustn't dream of it. Everything's under control."

"What about the Embassy? Won't they be upset?"

"They are, of course, but it's not as if Willa was still on the staff. Don't worry, Daddy. They'll look after me."

"Then when are you coming home?"

"When we've found Gustav."

"Who the devil's he?"

"Willa's lover. The one who got her in this fix."

"Well, he'd better face the music, hadn't he?"

But that's the last thing murderers do, Grace said to herself as she put the telephone down. Gustav wasn't likely to face any music, nor to come out from the shelter of his anonymity.

The two police officers paid a call that morning. They went over the flat silently, opening drawers, lifting things. The cause of death, said one, had now been established. Froken Bedford had died by drowning, but the high percentage of alcohol in her blood suggested one of three things. Either she had got drunk enough to give herself courage to wade into the icy water, she had fallen in accidentally, again because of her unsteady state, or she had not seriously resisted being pushed. The first eventuality was the most likely.

The police, with their practical minds, still regarded the diary as a fairly useless and unreal document. The only thing that interested them in it, apart from the identity of Gustav, was this place where Willa had complained of the forest and the rain dripping on the roof. It seemed highly probable that that was where she had spent her last days.

"Why do you ask me where it is?" Grace demanded. "I'm a stranger here."

The two men nodded in agreement. They seemed even less interested today than they had been yesterday in the enquiry. It was a routine suicide case. Dull.

Polsen insisted on taking Grace out to lunch. He was hungry, he said unashamedly. She would find she was, too, when she began to eat. Anyway, one had to escape from Fru Lindstrom who was doing her jack-in-the-box trick, not only popping out of her own door at the slightest sound, but appearing at Grace's, without apology.

She, of course, had expected this tragedy although she had never said so. Froken Bedford, for all her apparent worldliness, had been an innocent. Imagine trusting a man so completely! Fru Lindstrom had given up trusting men before she was twenty. Not that that meant that she didn't like them. But never should a girl be crazy enough to let a man break her heart.

She would like to see this Gustav. He must be really something. Two days the poor girl had been in the lake. Where had everyone been at that time?

"All that matters is where Gustav was," Grace said.

"Taking regard of who Gustav is," said Polsen. "Put your coat on, Grace. We're going out for some lunch, Fru Lindstrom."

"Good, good. Froken Asherton needs feeding. She has grown smaller since yesterday. She isn't much bigger than that canary." It was a pity Fru Lindstrom's laugh sounded quite so jolly. It seemed a little macabre.

They went across to the old town to a restaurant Polsen knew. It was just the place for a cold day, he said, in a cosy dark-panelled room with windows looking over the old square. By chance—was it by chance?—the door of Doctor Backe's house was just visible. Grace could see the coppery glint of the charming little dragon.

"So what were we all doing on Saturday evening," Polsen said. "I was driving back from Uppsala. I was alone. I have no witnesses. Then I spent the evening working on translations. Again alone."

"You don't have to tell me what you were doing," Grace said, her strained gaze on him.

"I prefer to. Now the rest. Axel? We don't know. Presumably he was worrying about getting his ship loaded. Sven?"

"He was home with his family. At least that was where Ebba and I left him after tea. And Jacob was with Ebba and me. Except—there was that conversation about Gustav attending to something."

242

"Yes. I had remembered that."

"Could he have been Willa's Gustav?"

"We don't know, do we? Who else? Peter Sinclair? We must include him. He is part of the circle."

"He was working late, Kate said. He'd had flu. He looked rather ill. All the men went shooting on Sunday, but by that time—" Grace couldn't eat, after all. She laid down her knife and fork, and said, "To think that when I was admiring all those pretty fawn-coloured rushes bending over the water, even then—"

"I share the opinion of the police, Grace," Polsen said, quietly ignoring her emotion. "We have to find where Willa was kept."

"A prisoner?"

"It seems so."

Grace leaned forward, speaking with intensity.

"Tell me I'm mad, if you like, but I'm certain some of the time she was in the attics at the von Sturpes. I have no proof except that bit of old fur. And that I think Ebba wanted me there to show me indirectly that the attics were empty. It's only a feeling I have. Don't laugh at me."

"I'm not laughing at you. Now look!"

Polsen was staring out of the window. "There's something happening."

"What?"

"Doctor Backe is leaving his house, carrying a fairly large briefcase. He can't be visiting a patient, with a briefcase, can he? He would have his doctor's bag. That's interesting." Polsen stood up. "Excuse me, Grace. I suddenly feel it's time I had a doctor look at my sinuses."

He disappeared, coming back a few minutes later to say what a pity, he couldn't make an appointment with Doctor Backe at present since the doctor had just left to attend a medical conference in Copenhagen. He had left no word as to when he would be back. In about a week, the nurse thought, but he has promised to telephone from Copenhagen.

"He didn't say anything about this at the weekend," Grace said in surprise.

"No, I expect not."

"*Is* there a conference in Copenhagen?"

"We can find that out easily enough. I would say there is. I don't think Doctor Backe would risk inventing that, but he had certainly made a last minute decision to attend it. I wonder why? Come, eat up your food. We must go."

244

One had to suppose it was a piece of luck discovering Sven Backe's activities, in this way. By another lucky chance, as they left the restaurant and walked down the narrow cobbled street, they encountered the nurse hurrying along. Sven must have told her she could go home for the remainder of the day. She was wrapped in a heavy tweed coat, and had on a shaggy fur hat that almost obliterated her small, unmemorable face. But not so much so that Grace didn't notice her eyes were red, from crying. Or else the bitter wind had reddened them.

What could Sven have told her? That he wasn't coming back?

PETER SINCLAIR was on the telephone a few minutes after they returned home. He had been ringing every ten minutes, he said. Where had Grace been?

"Out to lunch," she said, and he seemed both relieved and surprised.

"That's more sensible than my wife. She won't look at food. I was afraid the police might have dragged you off for some questioning."

"No, they came here instead."

245

"And have they found anything significant? In the diary, or elsewhere?"

"They don't seem particularly interested in the diary."

"They don't share your view that it's important?"

"No, they like facts, not fancies."

Peter laughed. "Willa was a great leg puller, you know."

"But it was her own leg that was pulled in the end, wasn't it?"

Peter's voice sobered. "You don't have to remind me, Grace. I was ringing, actually, to see if you could come out. I've got to be at the office, and Kate really has me worried. She's in such a state she's got the kids upset, too. I don't like leaving them with her. I wondered if you might be able to take them out for a couple of hours. I thought it would do you good, too. Get you out of that morbid flat."

Where the Embassy could keep an eye on her? Grace wondered.

"I'm not alone, Peter. Polsen's here."

"That fellow! Look here, how much do you know about him? How do you know he isn't another Gustav? Or *the* Gustav, even! Don't answer, I expect he's listening now, isn't he? But use a bit of caution, won't you, Grace?

And it would do the kids a lot of good to see you. They talk about you all the time. Take them for a walk on Gordit. It'll keep you all out of mischief."

Peter was certainly a man who had no inhibitions about giving orders. Grace wondered if this directive had come from higher up, or whether he spoke the plain truth when he said that Georgy and Alexander were frightened and miserable.

There was no alternative, she would have to go and find out, otherwise the anxious white faces of the children would haunt her.

"Good idea," said Polsen. "I'll drop you there, and pick you up again in a couple of hours."

"You probably guessed—Peter said I must be cautious, how much did I know about you?"

He came to stand over her, kissing her on the forehead.

"And how much do you?"

"Enough."

Grace scarcely knew why she was taken aback when the door of the Sinclairs' flat was opened by Ebba. That woman seems to be everywhere, she was thinking, as Ebba began to talk in a voice that was one agitated note higher than usual.

"Oh, Grace, I've been trying to telephone you. All yesterday, when I heard that you were in Uppsala—and again this morning."

When I was in Polsen's bed, Grace thought, gathering the warmth of that thought about her.

"Did you have anything to tell me?" she asked. It was much easier to be offhand with Ebba when one was no longer her guest.

"About Willa?"

"That would be all I would be interested in just at present."

"I haven't, of course. I only wanted to say how shocked and unhappy I am. I couldn't stay at home after the police had been."

"Why have they been to you?"

"They've been everywhere where Willa was known. The Backes, too. They frightened the old lady out of her wits." (That smug old woman with her white pillow hands. Nothing would frighten her. Or Ulrika. But Sven—did Ebba know he had crept away?)

"Who would have guessed Willa would do such a crazy thing?"

"Nobody," said Grace flatly.

The curious pale eyes flickered. "You don't agree that she took her own life?"

"Just because she was pregnant! Good heavens, no!"

"You don't think there might have been other reasons?"

"Not for suicide. I tell you, Willa just wasn't that type." She looked at Ebba levelly. "No matter what anybody had tried to do to her. I've told the police what sort of person she was. I'm glad they've been to see you. I did think it awfully funny the way her fur tie got in your attic."

Ebba frowned. "Why are you like this, Grace? So aggressive. I haven't harmed Willa."

Grace lifted her chin. "I'm aggressive to everybody just now. Willa's dead, and I can't believe it. I'm more angry than shocked. I can't think of any reason bad enough for her to have to die. But I'll find out what it was, I promise you that." She paused, and gave a half repentant shrug for her outburst. "I think some of Willa's got into me. Or else I was always more like her than I thought. Perhaps it's an improvement."

"Then be careful you don't go her way," Ebba said.

"Oh, I'll take care no one pushes me in a lake," Grace said deliberately. "If that's what you mean. Where's Kate?"

"She's lying down. I made her take a sedative. I came here after talking to Peter. He was worried about her. She's terribly sensitive, isn't she? How did you get here? By taxi?"

"Polsen drove me."

"Oh. Look, Grace—none of us know much about this Polsen. Are you sure you're not being too trusting?"

"Like Willa? No."

"You say that very definitely."

Anger boiled in Grace again.

"Of course I do. I don't want to hear you say anything about Polsen. I've come for the children. I'll go and get them."

The children hadn't come bursting down the stairs in their usual way. They were unnaturally silent. Someone must have told them to put on their outdoor things, for they were buttoned into woolly overcoats, and had on their tam-o'-shanters, Alexander's crooked, Georgy's crushed on to uncombed hair that hung in her eyes. Georgy, indeed, had shed all her belligerence and was holding Alexander's hand in the meekest way.

"Well! How come you're all dressed up?" Grace said cheerfully.

"Daddy said you were taking us out. Aren't you?"

"I am. We're walking on Gordit, I believe."

A flash of Georgy's spirit returned.

"You don't say Gordit, you say Yerdit."

"Oh. Do you know the way?"

"Of course we do. We've been hundreds of times."

"One day," said Alexander, "Daddy says we can have a puppy."

"Yes, you should have a dog to take for a walk," said Georgy.

This was true, for most of the people walking on the pleasant undulating parkland that stretched for several miles to include small inns and restaurants, and an inevitable arm of Lake Malaren, had dogs gambolling at their heels. They wore their habitual uniform of sober dark overcoats and scarves although today there was champagne-coloured sunshine that made the grass tawny and sparkling.

The children's spirits rose as their walk progressed. They were deeply interested in the story of the canary Polsen had given Grace.

251

"That's what I'd have if I didn't have a puppy," Alexander said.

"A puppy's better," said Georgy. "You can't take a bird for walks. It would fly away." Alexander giggled and made flapping movements with his arms, and Georgy went on, "Does Polsen like you, Grace?"

"It's rude to say Polsen, you should say Herre Polsen."

Georgy ignored Alexander, and persisted, "Does he, Grace? Does he want to marry you?"

"Now whatever gave you that idea?" Grace asked.

"Mummy says you're getting as bad as Willa, with men you don't know anything about, and Daddy says you should go back to England."

"I like Polsen," said Alexander.

"How do you know you do? You haven't seen him."

"I have. I saw him bring Grace in his car. I saw him kiss her goodbye. I thought only mothers and fathers are supposed to kiss."

"You are old-fashioned," said Grace. "Kissing's fun. As you'll find out one day."

"Ick!" said Georgy. "I saw Daddy and Ebba kissing once. Their lips were stuck together like this." She pushed out her lips exaggeratedly. "It looked as if they were starting to eat each other."

Alexander, wracked with giggles, had to stop to get his breath.

"You did not, Georgy! You're making it up."

"I am not. I'll show you how they kissed."

They were off, Georgy pursuing Alexander in circles over the shining grass. And Grace was thinking, Peter and Ebba. Was this at the bottom of Kate's unhappiness? If so, how did Peter have the nerve to preach to her about discretion with Polsen? In his position his own indiscretion would be flagrant.

It was only at the end of their walk that Willa was mentioned. Then Georgy, with her uncomfortable acumen, observed calmly, "I except Willa couldn't see where she was going because she had lost her glasses. That's how she came to fall in the lake."

KATE WAS UP and dressed and making tea when they returned. She looked ill, her face was sallow and her eyes sunken, and she fumbled with the cups and saucers, rattling them dangerously. But at least she was making an effort. There was no sign of Ebba.

"Grace, you are a love, taking the children out. They look ever so much better. I've had a rest and I feel better, too. We have been a dopey household. Peter's still not a bit well, but he insists on going to the office as usual. Especially now." Kate bit her lip, and seemed determined not to mention Willa. "You will stay to tea, won't you?"

"Polsen's calling for me at five o'clock. Have I time?"

"He can have some tea, too. We really haven't met him properly. I know Peter would like to. Children, go upstairs and wash. And did you thank Grace for your lovely walk?"

Something had detained Polsen. They had had their tea, and it was six o'clock and he still hadn't arrived. Peter came home, calling in a falsely jovial voice, "Hullo, Grace. Nice to have you here."

His joviality was quite a triumph, judging by his tired drained look. He still had a head cold and it had left his nose and lips swollen. Fleetingly, he reminded Grace of someone, she couldn't remember at the moment whom it was.

"This has been one hell of a week," he

said. "A dose of flu, a dose of overwork, and now Willa."

"Ebba was here," Kate said in an expressionless voice.

"I know. She came into the office, too. She's blaming herself. Like we all are."

"Why?" Grace asked.

"Well, for accepting Willa's story, for one thing. For not trying to find out more about the mysterious Gustav—"

"What's it to do with Ebba?" Kate interrupted.

"What it is to do with us all. We were friends. It's—"

"Hush! The children are coming. Don't discuss it in front of them."

"Could I telephone?" Grace asked. "I'm wondering what's happened to Polsen."

"Was he picking you up? I expect that old car of his has broken down. Is there any more tea, Kate? No, don't bother. I'll have whisky instead."

No one answered the telephone. Grace contemplated ringing Fru Lindstrom, then decided against it. No need to make a thing about Polsen being an hour late and have her clucking with a new drama. No need for her heart to begin its hard thudding of alarm. In a moment the doorbell would ring.

When another half hour had gone by, however, Grace had to confess to her uneasiness.

"Peter, would you drive me home? You don't mind, Kate?"

"Of course not. But where is Polsen? He doesn't seem very reliable."

"He is. You all keep telling me I don't know much about him, but reliability has always been one of his things."

"Willa said that about Gustav," Kate said. "Did you know? She stood in this room saying it. Didn't she, Peter?"

Peter stood up, saying briskly, "Sure, I'll take you, Grace. I don't know why we're all getting so doomy because a chap's unpunctual. Perhaps he's forgotten. The absent-minded professor, eh?"

13

IT was surely simple enough, Fru Lindstrom said. Herre Polsen had had a telephone call about four o'clock and had gone out. Fru Lindstrom wouldn't have known even that much if she had not been vigilant, as always, and caught him just as he was leaving the house. With all these untoward events she was nervous and liked to put the chain on the door at nights. So she had enquired how late Herre Polsen would be and he had said he would be back within an hour since he had promised to call for Froken Asherton and bring her home. The place of his appointment could not have been far off for his car was still outside, if they liked to look. What was the time now? Seven o'clock? Well, you knew what men were when they began having a few drinks.

"I'll come up with you," Peter said to Grace. "See everything's all right."

Inside Willa's flat it was he who shivered.

"I don't know, this place strikes me as

damned morbid now. You shouldn't stay here."

Grace spread the cover over the canary's cage. She knew that she was not going to stir one inch from here until Polsen returned. He would be back any minute. She would prepare a meal and open a bottle of wine. She didn't mind being alone, or waiting. She was used to waiting.

"For Willa? But she didn't come back," Peter said bluntly.

Grace turned on him. "Are you suggesting Polsen won't? One minute you're insisting that Willa's death was suicide, and the next you're telling me something sinister could happen on a perfectly ordinary afternoon in Stockholm."

All the same, her heart had that hard agitated beat again.

"Don't be utterly mad," she went on, trying to reassure herself with words. "I expect Polsen has gone to see his son. He's absolutely devoted to that boy. I think it's from conscience, as well as love. I mean, his marriage going wrong—" Her voice died away as she met Peter's intent gaze.

"You can't be suggesting he has a conscience over Willa, too!" she burst out incredulously.

"Or Willa's expected child?" said Peter flatly. "All right then, Grace, I'll leave you, since you insist. But you've got to get yourself a flight home the moment the police release the—I mean, arrangements are made about Willa. These are orders. Otherwise, you'll become *persona non grata*."

Grace stood quite still listening to Peter's footsteps going down the stairs. She thought she hated him, with his open boyish British face, and the monstrous thoughts he dropped into her mind.

The king with two queens . . . A man whose first wife, or second, had become an embarrassment to him . . .

By ten o'clock, after Fru Lindstrom had twice made the journey upstairs to see that Grace was all right (what did she expect to happen?) and when the house was too silent to endure, she picked up the telephone and rang the police.

"But I know he wouldn't go on some journey without telling me," she said. "He was to have picked me up at five o'clock. That's more than five hours ago. Yes, he *was* always a person to keep his word. In my experience he was utterly reliable. Only something serious would keep him out this late."

They said, somewhat indifferently, that they would make a routine check. Perhaps Fru Polsen could tell them something.

"Fru—" Grace began, and stopped. Polsen's wife had never been a reality, until now. She didn't care for it.

"Please tell me if you find out anything," she begged.

An hour later the sergeant telephoned. "No luck, Froken Asherton," he reported. "Fru Polsen hasn't seen or heard from her husband today, and he hasn't been to the university. However, for what it's worth, one of his students saw him in the old town this afternoon."

"But that was with me. We had lunch."

"No, later. About four o'clock. Would he be visiting anyone there, to your knowledge?"

"Only Doctor Backe, but he's left for Copenhagen. We saw him go."

"Copenhagen, eh?"

"There's a medical conference there. He was going to it."

"Ah. That might be interesting."

"It's Herre Polsen, not Doctor Backe I want to find," Grace pointed out.

"*Ja.* Leave it to us, Froken Asherton. We'll find them both."

That, considering Willa, sounded far too glib. Meanwhile they hadn't told her how the night was to be lived through. Surely Polsen would come home. If he didn't—but where would he be, if he didn't, or couldn't, come home?

Grace made some tea, decided to take a shower to refresh herself and pass some time, then dressed again, and paced up and down. Once she went up to Polsen's room, thinking he might have crept in quietly without her hearing. But that room, like her own, was full of the now familiar crushing silence. *Where* was Polsen?

In the early hours the wind began to whine against the windows again. The sound was like a whip on her raw nerves. She sat with her hands pressed against her ears, too tense, too miserable for tears. It was the loneliest night that she had ever spent.

Early in the morning there was another telephone call from the police. It had been ascertained that Doctor Sven Backe had not been a passenger on any flight from Stockholm, to Copenhagen or elsewhere. Was Grace sure of the accuracy of her information?

"Ask his nurse," Grace said, her voice taut with weariness. "Haven't you found out anything about Herre Polsen?"

"Not yet. Sorry, froken. Sometimes a man comes home in time for breakfast."

Grace slammed down the receiver, quivering with rage at the unfeeling facetiousness of that thick-necked and thick-skulled policeman.

She made more tea, drinking it with a kind of desperation. It was eight o'clock and still dark. What was she to do all day? What was she to do if Polsen didn't come back?

"Grace! Grace!"

The whisper from the door startled her out of her wits. She hadn't realised she had left her door unlocked. She certainly was not expecting Winifred Wright at this hour.

"I knocked but you didn't hear. Sorry to barge in like this, but there's something I want to tell you. At least, something I think you ought to know. I don't suppose you could make some coffee. I rushed off without a thing, I thought I might get cautious and

262

change my mind if I waited. God knows, enough wild rumours go about."

Winifred was flushed, and had a dishevelled look, as if she had thrown her clothes on, and left her hair uncombed. Grace, for all her curiosity, found she had a strange reluctance to hear this information which Winifred was in such a hurry to impart.

She went into the kitchen to put the coffee on, saying over her shoulder, "Is it about Willa? Or Polsen?"

"Polsen? What's he got to do with it?"

"He didn't come home last night. I'm worried about him." She gave a dry laugh. "Worried is hardly the word. I'm really a little demented."

Winifred came to the kitchen door. Now her large creased plump face was full of concern.

"Does he usually tell you where he goes?"

"Lately, yes. We—" Grace's voice caught with emotion. "Hell, is there a hoodoo on this place? Everyone disappears!"

"You've got nervous. Waiting so long for Willa, and then—"

"Polsen isn't in the lake!" Grace said vehemently. "Don't you suggest that."

"Good lord, no. Who would have the strength to drown him?"

The bleak ugly words came out before Winifred could stop them. She said quickly, "I didn't mean that, Grace. He'll be all right. Be back any minute. My, that coffee smells good. No, it's something about Willa I wanted to tell you. You know that she wore an antique ring, an enormous thing too big for her hands really."

"Yes, the police showed it to me." With the little pile of crumpled clothing, the water-sodden shoes, the gold watch that had been a twenty-first birthday present and the bracelet with its clinking collection of good luck charms. The ring, with its dark blue stone and baroque setting, had looked medieval, as if the donor had selected it with care from among his family heirlooms.

"What's its significance?" she asked.

"It wasn't an engagement ring, although Willa pretended it was. I don't think Gustav ever gave her anything, so she had to pretend."

Grace stared. "Then who did give it to her? Do you know?"

"I think so. I think it was Peter Sinclair."

"Peter!"

"And I think Kate knows. That's why she's in such a state."

"Peter!" Grace breathed again. "But why? You don't think he was having an affair with her?"

"I would have thought it extremely unlikely. He's too ambitious, for one thing. He wouldn't have risked his career by getting involved with his secretary. And for another, she really wasn't his type. She used to exasperate him to fury. He was going to ask to have her transferred to another department if she hadn't decided to leave."

"But she was always at the Sinclairs."

"Kate liked her. She was gay and amusing and good with the children. And when she first came to Stockholm I think she did have a bit of a crush on Peter, but no one took any notice of that because she flirted with every man in sight."

"Then why on earth give her a ring, an expensive one at that!"

"I only know Willa's story. At the farewell party we gave her, I found her in the ladies' room crying. Mind you, she'd had too many drinks. She'd been trying to fix her face, and had left the ring lying on the washbasin. I picked it up, and said 'Gustav wouldn't like you to lose this.' She took it from me, saying that actually she didn't care for it very much and only wore it so as not to hurt Peter's feelings."

"She was drunk, she made a mistake."

"No, she didn't, because she realised what she'd said, and was frightfully embarrassed. She begged me not to tell anybody. The truth was, Gustav hadn't given her a ring yet, he was going to when they were married, but she didn't want people to think he was mean so she pretended this one was his. She had seen it in a jewellers' and had longed for it so much that Peter had helped her pay for it. He said it could be a gift for all her baby-sitting, but not to tell Kate. He didn't mind her pretending it was her engagement ring—only in Embassy circles, of course."

"What an extraordinary story!" Grace said. "I can't believe it."

"Neither could I, to tell the truth. I still don't know what's fact and what isn't, because Willa really was pretty drunk that night, and she was good at inventing stories at any time."

"But if she wanted the ring so much why did she then say she hated it?"

"Goodness knows. Because she secretly wanted diamonds, probably."

Grace nodded. That made sense. Willa had always had a habit of wanting something overpoweringly, and then, when she had got it, of wanting something better. It was her power complex, she said.

"And Kate knows this story?"

"I'm not sure. She may only suspect it. She hasn't got much confidence, poor Kate. I've noticed her looking at Ebba von Sturpe lately as if she doesn't trust her."

And with reason, if she had seen the kiss that Georgy talked about. Poor Kate, indeed. Peter seemed to be a bit of a philanderer. He would have to be more careful if he really was so ambitious about his career.

But this strange story of that ring that must have weighed down Willa's hand as she sank in the Lake. Like a stone tied round her neck. What did it all mean? And why wasn't Polsen here to rationalise it for her?

"Does this make things any more clear?" Winifred asked.

"As clear as mud," Grace said hopelessly.

"Will you tell the police?"

"I'm not sure. How significant is it? I'd hate Kate to get hurt. And the children.

They're too sharp at sensing things. I'll have to think. Thanks, anyway, Winifred. Thanks for coming. I'm getting absolutely morbid about being alone."

Don't sit there brooding, Grace said to herself, when Winifred had gone. Do something. Ring Peter and have it out with him about that ring. Find out from the police if they have any clues about Polsen. Dear God, let him be all right. See if that love-sick nurse is at Doctor Backe's and cross-examine her about the conference in Copenhagen.

There were plenty of constructive things to do, especially now that a tardy sun was coming up, and the canary was beginning to twitter, preparatory to bursting into full song. Polsen would have said that it was just a day like any other, not the end of the world. Well, one had to find out about that.

Peter's voice was surprised, then decidedly wary. Or was she imagining that?

"That lapis lazuli ring? *What* story have you heard? No, don't tell me. This isn't a thing to talk about on the telephone. I'll come and see you. Give me an hour. I must clear my desk up a bit. It looks like a dog's breakfast. Okay?"

He rang off abruptly. Grace was mildly

satisfied with her first result. She was making things happen. Now for the love-sick nurse.

This conversation began tentatively. She had difficulty in making the girl realise who she was, and it wasn't until she mentioned Willa's name that there was a gasp at the other end, and the girl said, after a silence, "What do you want to know?"

"I wanted to come and see Doctor Backe, but I hear he's gone to Copenhagen."

"*Ja.*"

"Did he fly?"

"I don't know. His car has gone. He may have driven to Malmo."

"Did he say when he would be back?"

"No. I should think in a week—actually—"

"Actually what?"

The voice lost its stiffness and began to tremble.

"Actually I'm worried. He took things. His microscope, for example. As if—"

"As if he weren't coming back?" Grace prodded.

There was a stifled sob. "That's what I'm afraid of. For some time now—no, I mustn't talk. But yesterday, after he had said goodbye and told me to go home, he came back."

"And you hadn't gone home?"

Grace remembered vividly seeing the thin figure with the red eyes wheel about and run back to the house with the dragon door-knocker.

"No, I was rather upset. I thought I would spend the afternoon working, after all. There were accounts . . ." Her voice trailed off.

"So you heard Doctor Backe come back?"

"Yes. Since he found me there he asked me to make a telephone call. To Herre Polsen. Then we waited, and Herre Polsen came, and—"

Grace managed to say calmly, "Go on."

"They were upstairs for a little while. Then the Baron and Baroness von Sturpe came, and they were all upstairs. And then they all went away."

"Polsen, too?"

"*Ja.* I saw a white car at the end of the street. There aren't many white Mercedes in Stockholm."

Polsen, you fool, you've been lured into something! What, for God's sake!

"Thank you," Grace said quickly. "You've been a great help."

The girl was crying again.

"Froken Asherton, do you think he will come back?"

270

"Doctor Backe? Why not? If he's only gone to a conference."

"But it's more than that. You must know it is."

There was no time to reassure the unfortunate creature, who was going to have her heart broken whether Sven returned or not. Grace had to make an urgent call to the police.

Strangely enough, they had been about to contact her, they said. They thought they had discovered the cottage where Froken Bedford had spent her last days. There were some articles that Grace might help them to identify. They would like her to come at once. It was only an hour's drive. Could she be ready in ten minutes? They could talk in the car.

At last the waiting was over. Grace flung on her outdoor things, warm coat, scarf, fur hat. It would be cold, in spite of the fragile sunlight. She remembered to scribble a note and leave it for Peter. That business about the ring would have to wait. Perhaps it wouldn't matter any more when she returned. She was so sure, although for no valid reason, that Polsen would have got to the cottage first, and be there waiting for them.

She was wrong about Polsen, but right in

her intuition that the cottage they were speeding towards was the Sinclairs, because one went down the same tracks all the time in this strange game. There it stood in the little clearing, the forest, now that clouds had lowered, darker than ever. It was familiar, almost like home, as it must have been to Willa even though the rain got on her nerves.

"You have been here before?" said the police officer.

"Yes. How do you know?"

"You don't seem surprised."

"Nothing surprises me any more."

She hadn't told the police about the ring Peter had given Willa. That could wait. She had, however, told them word for word her conversation with the girl at Doctor Backe's, and after listening in silence one of the men had given some incomprehensible instructions on the car radio. A little later the radio had answered back. The only word Grace could understand was Gothenburg. Did they think that was where Polsen was?

She asked, and was told no, this was another matter. But interesting, nevertheless.

So, irrationally, her hopes rose that Polsen might be at the cottage.

Of course he was not. It was empty and

silent and filled with a strange odour. Grace wrinkled her nose.

"Smells like something burnt. Wool?"

"Right, froken. You would make a good detective, *ja*?"

The hearth was swept clean, too clean. But there was a very small pile of carefully gathered sweepings on a sheet of paper. There was also, more disturbingly, a suitcase encrusted with dried mud on the floor.

One of the policemen opened it and Grace's hand went to her mouth. It was full of women's clothing, and even if she hadn't recognised one candy-striped blouse she had frequently seen Willa wear, she must have guessed whom these forlorn garments belonged to.

"This guilty person," she was told with the quaint formality of the sergeant's English, "began by burning Froken Bedford's possessions. But that was going to take too long. Wool, for one thing, is difficult to burn. So he dug a hole near the wood-heap and buried this bag, and the half-burnt garments. Then he piled the wood over the mound and hoped for snow."

"Why for snow?"

"If these things had been buried beneath

six feet of snow we wouldn't have found them until the spring. When, of course, we would no longer be looking for them. *Ja*, it was bad luck for this villain that the snow hasn't yet begun."

It was horribly cold in here, dank and cold.

"So now it's murder."

"*Ja*."

"How horrible," Grace whispered. After a little while she said sharply, "What do you want me here for? Haven't I looked at Willa's things enough?"

"You can identify these?"

"Some," she said reluctantly.

"Good." The man smartly closed the case. Then he said unexpectedly, "The diary. You say you found it in the birdcage. Your cousin was clever at hiding places. Here, for instance, she left another diary which escaped the notice of the person who thought he had cleared everything up tidily. We found it under the clock. Just here. So simple, isn't it?"

Grace looked fascinatedly at the small pigskin pocket diary.

"What's in it? More riddles?"

"Riddles?" The officer, who was growing quite endearing with his solemn eyes and earnest desire to understand English, didn't know this word. "We don't know what's in it. We want you to read it for us. The script is very small and difficult, but you understand your cousin's handwriting?"

Grace looked at the spiky writing crushed into the small pages. Her heart was beating too fast again. What was this? Another cryptogram?

It seemed to be a real diary with entries under their proper dates, but the entries grew longer and longer, running over several days at a time. The writing was so cramped as to be almost illegible. The last sentence was unfinished. Willa must have been interrupted. She must, by then, have been in terror of whoever had interrupted her. But she had still found an opportunity to slide the little book under the clock. It was her last mute cry for help.

"Sit down, froken," said the officer. "And please speak slowly so that I can make notes."

Grace obeyed, poring over the little book, reading in a stiff voice.

3 October. Peter waiting for me at railway station as he had promised. Good idea to let that nosey Fru Lindstrom and others think I

was leaving by train. We got in car and drove very fast. Very happy. Laughed all the time. Wondered if I had been a bit mad to write that letter to Grace. But thinking of Bill, I guessed a bit of caution wasn't a bad idea. Am I awful to still love Peter?

5 October. Two days of bliss. Peter supposed to be having a weekend elk-shooting. But now he's gone back to Stockholm and I feel a bit gloomy. It's this early dark, and I keep hearing the forest rustling. Makes me think of Bill. So I'll write what led up to this, to pass the time.

Why do men confide in me so often? Bill said I was simpatico. Poor devil. He was terribly worried and rather drunk. Fancy, he told me he was being got at by a Russian agent because the Russians had these pornographic photographs of him. He had a Swedish boy friend. You'd never have guessed he was that type. I bet the Ambassador didn't know. Of course they had to make his death an accident, but I knew it was suicide. I had it on my mind so much that I told Peter, but he ordered me to keep my mouth shut. There mustn't be a scandal. I realised that, of course. Realised Peter and I would have to be discreet too. We fell in love the week after Bill's death, that hot summer day by the lake when I told him Bill's story. I'd adored Peter from the start, but I didn't know he had me. He said he had been unhappy with Kate for a long time, but I must give him time to work that out. It isn't fair for him to be unhappy because he's so marvellous when he's happy.

Anyway, soon after we knew we were in love, he persuaded me to leave Winifred's flat and get one of my own which he found for me. Things were just fine, we had a great time, until I got pregnant.

Honestly I didn't mean to, I don't play those tricks. But when I knew this had happened I wouldn't listen to Peter's suggestions about an abortion. I wasn't going to be a murderess again. I told him how I'd nearly had a mental breakdown after my first abortion. This time I intended to have my baby. I wanted it, especially since it was his. We went to the cottage and spent a whole day arguing. I wouldn't budge an inch. I felt sorry for Peter because this would be tough on his career but he should have thought of that in the first place. I intended to have my baby, and him, too. He says I have a ruthless streak. This is true, but you've got to fight for things in this life.

Anyway, that was the day when the awful, the cataclysmic thing happened. Peter went out to get some wood for the fire, and I wanted a cigarette and got his silver case out of his jacket that he'd left lying on the bed. I hadn't handled the case before, so I'd never had the chance to find the sort of flap that shut off a secret compartment. Of course I looked in it, I'm as nosey as Fru Lindstrom, and there was this thin bit of paper with bits of potted history of several people in the Embassy and things like 'weakness for blue films' or 'a pushover with women' underlined.

I couldn't believe it at first. It *couldn't* be Peter who had told the Russian agent things about Bill Jordan. But it must have been. My Peter! I really love this man. Even knowing this I still love him. You can't cut off emotions in a split second. After all Melinda Maclean followed her husband, didn't she? And later married another spy, Philby.

Was Peter really a spy? I couldn't work that out. All I knew was that I had here, in my hands, a means of making him marry me. And I was going to use it. I knew I was. My baby deserved a legitimate father, didn't it?

Am I awful? Am I as bad as Peter for

278

betraying Bill? But I really am mad about him. When he takes me to bed I couldn't care the faintest bit about anything else in the whole world. He's a man and I'm a woman and that's all there is to it. Communists, anti-communists. What are they?

It's only when I sit here in the half dark listening to the forest rustling, and wondering how long it will take him to get Kate and the kids sent back to England (where they want to go, anyway), and his resignation given in. (We've planned to go to Germany, probably Munich. Peter speaks perfect German, and he'll get a job there.)

But to go back to that evening. It was pretty painful. We drank a lot of schnapps and I cried, and Peter said of course he loved me, but this was all crazy and I was jumping to conclusions, those notes were quite harmless. However, I didn't budge an inch. After all, I'd talked to Bill, and it was from this cottage that he'd gone out and shot himself. Truly I never want to see the place again, and I *loathe* being here alone.

Well, anyway, Peter realised that even if no one believed my story it was going to do him a lot of harm, so finally he gave in. We'd get married when he'd got a divorce. We'd go back to Stockholm that night and I'd give notice at work and say I was getting married to a Swede. We'd have to give him a name, though, and we decided on Gustav, which I'd called Peter since that day at Gripsholm Castle.

He bought me a ring, this great lump of lapis lazuli that I adore. I swanked it around, and gave a party, and asked everybody, even that cold-eyed Axel. And Peter, to keep people from suspecting about us, made too much fuss of Ebba, and Kate was mad. So was I, although I couldn't say so.

And that's how I come to be sitting here in the dark, brooding. Since Peter has been rather naughty (although he still doesn't admit he's done anything wrong), I suppose I have to pay, too, by being lonely and miserable. And a bit frightened. After all, I'm condoning his misdeeds. Bill's dead because of him. Oh hell, why do I have to be left *here*?

16 October. Thank God, Peter came back this weekend. Said Grace was in Stockholm making a nuisance of herself. (Why did I write that letter? But I can't help feeling rather glad I did because I still might need a lifeline.) Peter couldn't stay long. Hadn't told

anyone he was coming here. But I'd be pleased to hear that Ebba and Jacob von Sturpe knew the whole story, were extremely sympathetic, and I was to go there for a while. So long as I promised to keep out of sight!

Now how could he have dared to tell Ebba and Jacob? Unless they are in this conspiracy with the Russians, too. Are they?

Now I'm glad Grace is here, makes me feel more secure. And a change of scene, as Peter said, will be good for me, although Ebba isn't my favourite person.

18 October. At Ebba's, but in the attics! She has asked me never to come down if there's anyone about. I was horrified when I found that I was being locked in. I rattled on the door until Ebba came and said not to be stupid, this was for *my* safety, not theirs. Why is being pregnant and waiting for one's lover to get a divorce such a *secret* affair? I thought the Swedes didn't give a hoot about these things. Of course, it all gets back to the Embassy, and the importance of no scandals. Blast them. I sit here and mope and slowly die of boredom.

20 October. They have asked me, Ebba and

Peter, to write to Grace. She is being awkward. Must reassure her. I am secretly maliciously pleased to sign my private signature that only Grace understands. Now she'll ask more questions than ever. Hear she found my dark glasses that I lost when I was staying in the cottage. I could have found them myself if I'd bothered, but who cares about that gimmick now. Any more than I care about my hair looking frightful now that the dye is fading. If Peter isn't careful I'll soon stop caring about looking attractive for him. This is the oddest treatment any bride ever got.

21 October. Have a fearful suspicion. It's that Peter hasn't given up this horrible business of telling tales to this mysterious agent, and I'm sure now that Ebba and Jacob are in it, too. That's why it was safe to bring me here. I'm beginning to hate Ebba. She was always cold. Now she's like a white snake, the way she writhes her long neck. Jacob is her cat's-paw, or whatever you call silly doting old men. I'm so tired of eating alone when they're entertaining. One day I'll start screaming. That'll startle the guests. Only, if I do anything silly, I'll lose Peter. I *must* be patient.

22 October. Today I swear I heard Axel Morgensson's voice downstairs. Is he in this, too? I have to stand on a chair to look out of these damned attic windows. By craning my head I did manage to see who was leaving, Axel *and* Sven Backe. So that's why Sven didn't like me asking him those questions about Bill Jordan's death? Now I'm glad I wrote all these names in the notes I left for Grace. I only had an intuition about them then, but I was right. Oh, God, when will I get out of here and get a wedding ring on my finger?

23 October. Ebba comes in and smiles and says 'Dear child, be patient. We're protecting you. If you do anything silly it will rebound on Peter, you know.' What silly thing could I do, except jump out of the window?

She's given me wool to knit baby things. When all the time I believe she would rather strangle my baby.

24 October. Such a thing, today—Ebba for once forgot to lock the door and I crept downstairs and telephoned Peter. Not at the office, at home. Georgy answered and didn't know what I was going on about, but she'll

tell her father and he'll come. Surely he'll come. Ebba caught me, and she was furious. She said that was the end, my not being trustworthy, and now I wouldn't even be allowed down for meals with her and Jacob when they were alone. Can't say I think that much of a penance. Except that I'm so lonely I'm going mad. What *is* Peter up to?

26 October. Peter is coming for me, hurray, hurray, hurray! Ebba has just been to tell me. Axel was here today back from a voyage. Was it his idea that Peter should take me away? Now I'm remembering that it was he who told Peter about the empty flat in Fru Lindstrom's house. It was just after I'd been to Sven and asked all those questions about Bill Jordan. I believe Axel wanted to keep his nasty staring eyes on me. Is he the one Peter told secrets to? Oh God, this is a mess.

27 October. Back at the old address. Peter cold and unfriendly. Won't talk about us getting married. I don't believe he has said a word to Kate. He is out now getting firewood. If he is expecting his usual evening by the fire with a bottle of schnapps, then off back to Stockholm leaving me here going

crazy, he's mistaken. Was he joking when he talked about a sea trip on Axel's ship? But it goes to the antarctic. All those icebergs. It couldn't be a pleasure trip. I'm going to politely decline that suggestion. Politely! Peter hasn't seen me when I'm really mad. Tonight he's going to find out, and if that doesn't convince him—

That was the end. That was when she had heard Peter coming, and had slid the little book under the clock. Grace felt cold to the bone.

"So Willa was the cargo Axel was waiting for," she said. "She was to be taken that day Jacob and Sven and Peter were supposed to be elk-shooting. But they found her gone. Peter must have had to put on an act since he was the one who knew exactly where she was. But he was good at putting on acts, wasn't he?"

"*Ja!* I imagine Herre Sinclair's friends were angry with him for making a mess of that job. He can't have expected the opposition the young lady put up."

"She fell into a lake instead of the sea with icebergs. But how could she have been persuaded to go down to the lake?"

"There was the empty schnapps bottle, and

the young lady a bit helpless by then, I expect. She was carried down and put in the rowing boat, and rowed out to a deeper part of the lake. A drink for you, froken?"

Grace lifted her frozen face.

"No, don't worry, I'm all right."

The police officer was calm, even a little contemptuous. "It's all a very small-scale affair compared to what might happen in Berlin, for instance. The Baroness von Sturpe came from East Germany, perhaps you knew. She is a very unpleasant woman and we know now that she has corrupted many people, including her husband who was a good man, but weak. She has a fatal power over men, including Herre Sinclair who was ready to betray his colleagues for her. And for money, of course. He is a greedy man. Your cousin was greedy, too. She enjoyed the presents Herre Sinclair gave her."

"All those people Willa tried to warn us about," Grace said. "Axel, Jacob, Sven, Gustav." She still didn't quite believe the revelation about Gustav's identity, although now she recalled sharply wondering whom Peter had reminded her of yesterday when his lips were swollen from his cold, his eye-lids heavy. Polsen would have spotted Gustav, she thought. And suddenly Willa was no longer uppermost in her mind.

"Polsen!" she cried in despair. "They've got him now. He went to Sven's house. Oh, God!"

A heavy hand came down on her shoulder.

"Don't worry, your friend will be all right. For instance," that phrase, which the officer obviously liked, was becoming monotonous, "we had news on the radio as we came here that Captain Morgensson's ship had put into Gothenburg. Presumably some cargo it had failed to pick up in Stockholm was now available. Or its—" he groped for the word, and the sergeant produced it, an air of pride in his knowledge. "Equivalent," he said.

"Unfortunately," said the officer, "there are often innocent victims in these affairs. But your friend Polsen won't be one. Neither will you. Come, we'll take you home."

It was dark now. The forest on either side of the long road was as black as a nightmare. Only in the headlights of the car could one see the whirling leaves.

"Look," said the sergeant, pointing to the windscreen. Untidy white blotches were spattering against it. "The snow is beginning," he said.

287

FOR ONCE, thank goodness, Fru Lindstrom was absent from her post in the hall. Weary to the bone, Grace climbed the stairs. She had refused the offer of the sergeant to accompany her.

"What is there to be afraid of now?" she had asked.

All the same, when she saw the door slightly ajar and the lights on, she was rigid. Who was in there? Peter Sinclair, with that strained look of frenzy in his blue eyes, waiting to take revenge?

Don't be a fool, if someone wanted to take you unawares the light wouldn't be on, she said to herself, firmly pushing the door open.

"So," said Polsen.

She flew into his arms. His thick jersey smelt of brine. His arms almost cracked her bones. When she looked up she saw that he wasn't wearing his glasses, and his mild blue eyes were full of ridiculous tears. There was a bruise down one cheek, and a neat cross of sticking plaster on his forehead.

"Polsen, you're hurt!"

"This bit of damage? It's nothing. Why are we crying?"

"It's you who's crying. Where are your glasses?"

"They got broken, unfortunately. Now, I know you're cold and you're tired, and my face is spoilt and I'm half blind without my glasses, but all the same we're going out to dinner at the nicest place there is."

"Are we celebrating something?" Grace asked in disbelief.

"Yes. Being alive. And free. I, for my own stupidity, nearly am not. Imagine being taken in by a telephone call. And from that girl we thought a ninny."

"What girl?"

"Doctor Backe's nurse. She said she had something important to tell me that couldn't be said on the telephone. She had been ordered to do this, of course. And when I got there, her master, her lover, whatever he is, was there also. And then Ebba and Jacob came. Although I'm a strong man I wasn't strong enough to overcome three people who had only one idea, to stick a hypodermic needle into my arm."

"And then?"

"Before I got quite unconscious I was helped into a car, a sick man being taken to hospital, anyone watching would think. And after that I knew nothing until the police stopped the car in Gothenburg. This was some time the next day, I am told."

"On the wharves?"

"So you know that?"

"Yes. You were going to be taken in Axel's ship behind the Iron Curtain. The interfering professor. Oh, Polsen! You risked your life for Willa."

"Not exactly for Willa. You're not as stupid as that, Grace. Now hurry with your bath. I'm hungry."

IT WAS STRANGE how the pretty bedroom didn't seem so cold now. It was almost warm and alive. Grace thought she would put on her red dress, then wondered if that was being heartless. "It's a gorgeous colour, Grace," she heard Willa saying. "Go on, wear it."

"Polsen," she called, "what happened to the others?"

"I understand the Baron and Baroness von Sturpe have been reported heading for the Finnish border. They won't be allowed over, of course. There will be some trouble with their passports. The brave Doctor Backe was found hiding in his sister's bedroom with his sister guarding the door and his thesis, which

290

he wanted published in Leningrad, in his briefcase. He had been planning to go, not to Copenhagen, but to Moscow, until Ebba sent him back with orders to lure me to his rooms. Last, Captain Morgensson has been taken off his ship and held for questioning."

"Not last, Peter Sinclair's last," Grace said bitterly.

"His wife and children were put on a flight for London late this afternoon. I can tell you that. The children were happy and excited about the flight, I heard."

"Polsen, *thank* you!"

"Sinclair himself is at the Embassy. That's out of our hands, of course. I believe the Ambassador wants to see you tomorrow. But that's tomorrow. Hurry up, Grace. Are you dressed? Am I to come and help you?"

"Going out without your glasses," Grace fretted.

"*Ja.* You will have to be my eyes."

The restaurant, the Teatro Grillen, was warm and cosy with its red walls, its dangling puppets and theatrical costumes. It reminded Grace reassuringly, even pleasantly, that sometimes life could be theatrical. Though not necessarily a constant melodrama, as Willa, with her restless nature, had made it.

Polsen's eyes, so much more obviously tender without the screen of the thick glasses, met hers over the candlelight.

"Champagne," he said firmly. "We have to drink to a beginning, not an end."

Her heart was jumping again, but not this time in alarm or cold fear.

"You wouldn't talk the other morning, Polsen."

"This is different."

"Emotion recollected in tranquillity," Grace murmured, and was pleased that he recognised the quotation.

"*Ja*. My emotion began when we went to Gripsholm, if you would like to know the exact moment."

"Looking for Gustav. And we always thought he had to be a Swede. Otherwise I think I would have seen him in Peter's face earlier. Do you think Ebba was in love with Peter?"

"That woman? She has never been in love with anything but power and intrigue and herself."

"But he was with her. I suppose he was flattered at the beginning. After all, he was quite ordinary and only a minor diplomat. She, with her elegance and sophistication and her position must have completely dazzled him. After all, admit it, Kate is a bit dreary."

"He was a puppet like those," said Polsen, pointing to the dangling puppets on the walls. "Don't waste any sympathy on him, Grace. He was stupid and gullible, he betrayed a colleague for money and sex, and was completely callous to his wife and children. He didn't even deserve Willa's inconvenient passion. Or perhaps he did, since it was fatal to him in the end. Spying in the grand manner for political beliefs is a corrupting enough profession, but in this nasty furtive low blackmailing way it is simply beneath contempt. So shall we talk of other things?"

But Grace had to probe her pain a little more.

"I suppose Willa deserved her end, too. She was stupid enough. And thoughtless and immoral. She never thought of what she was doing to Kate, and Georgy and Alexander." She sighed deeply. "Yes, let's talk of other things. Tell me about Magnus."

"Oh, he's fine," Polsen said enthusiastically. "He's got into the football team. He's a strong fellow. Can I bring him to see you on Sunday?"

"Polsen, that's the first time you've suggested that," Grace said in delight. "I thought you were keeping him away from me."

"Naturally. Small boys require straightforward things, such as us knowing we belong to each other."

"Do we?"

"Indubitably!"

"Oh, Polsen! You professor, with your long words. But I must go back to England first. I must talk to my father, my publishers, sort myself out."

"Of course, I understand. When will you be back?"

Not if, when. Polsen, like his son, had a direct mind.

"By Christmas?" she said tentatively.

He gave his shy beaming smile.

"Splendid. You will still be in time for the snow."

But she was in time now. For when they left the restaurant the streets were white with a crisp crunching coverlet. The wind was blowing the last ragged leaves from the trees, and the air, whirling with snowflakes, had become intensely clean and invigorating. Grace thought of the suddenly transformed pure white forests, the frozen lakes, the immaculate fields. She laughed with excitement and tucked herself close against Polsen's broad sheltering body.

THE END